Winter Escapes

Around the world in four romances!

Pack your bags and leave the postfestivity blues behind! This January, Harlequin Romance presents a whirlwind tour to some stunning international locations—and we want you to join us. Whether you're looking for sun, sea or snow, we've got you covered. So let yourself be swept away by these beautiful romances and discover how four couples make it to their true destination... happy-ever-after!

Get ready for the trip of a lifetime with...

Their Hawaiian Marriage Reunion
by Cara Colter

Copenhagen Escape with the Billionaire
by Sophie Pembroke

Prince's Proposal for the Canadian Cameras
by Nina Singh

Cinderella's Moroccan Midnight Kiss
by Nina Milne

All available now!

Dear Reader,

As a child I loved fairy tales, and as I grew up, while I did realize that perhaps it was a little more complicated than the books suggested, I still believed in the possibility of happy-ever-afters. So I loved the idea of writing a Cinderella story. However, Lily and Darius had other ideas; neither of them believed in happy-ever-afters, so they kept putting metaphorical pumpkins in the way. They needed to believe in themselves before love could weave its magic. I hope you enjoy reading their story to find out how they got past the pumpkins and made it to their happy-ever-after.

Nina x

CINDERELLA'S MOROCCAN MIDNIGHT KISS

NINA MILNE

ROMANCE

Harlequin®
ROMANCE

ISBN-13: 978-1-335-21628-1

Cinderella's Moroccan Midnight Kiss

Copyright © 2025 by Nina Milne

Harlequin Enterprises ULC
22 Adelaide St. West, 41st Floor
Toronto, Ontario M5H 4E3, Canada
www.Harlequin.com

Printed in U.S.A.

To my family.

CHAPTER ONE

LILY CULPEPPER GLARED down at her phone and read the message again.

Reminder! Countdown! Ten days to go! Until... Cynthia's hen break—a sun-soaked, cocktail-filled beach break in Gran Canaria. Let's send Cynthia off into marital bliss in style! Can't wait to see you again! Julia

Followed by a string of emojis.

Lily closed her eyes, then reopened them in the hope the message had miraculously disappeared. But of course, it hadn't. After all, the original invitation hadn't vanished, nor the first reminder, so realistically it was unlikely this one would comply.

There had to be a way out of this. It was bad—no, *horrendous*—enough that she had to go to Cynthia and Tom's Valentine's Day wedding, a ceremony in which her stepsister was going to marry Lily's ex.

It was a plotline worthy of a soap opera, and remembered humiliation washed over her in a flood of mortification at the thought of the scene—two years before, on Valentine's Day no less—when Tom had rejected her in favour of the stepsister who had made her childhood a misery.

Stop. She would not take that trip down memory lane. She would not relive the pain, the sear of rejection, the sheer disbelief. And she would not show anyone that she cared; instead, she would attend the wedding, smile, laugh and act as though she was totally on board. As though the heartbreak and betrayal had never happened.

But the prospect of the hen break triggered a different sense of panic engendered by a different set of memories. Memories of a boarding school where her life had been made miserable by her stepsisters and their cohort of 'friends' and acolytes. Now she would be trapped on a 'sun-soaked' island with the same people.

Not that anyone else seemed to have given it a thought. Apparently it was all forgotten, or at least water under the bridge—a bridge constructed by others. The general consensus seemed to be that, whilst their actions had been regrettable, they'd also somehow been justifiable. After all, Lily's mum had stolen Cynthia and Gina's dad, broken up a marriage and ruined their lives. All of which might be true, but that wasn't Lily's fault, though sometimes, in some surreal way, it had felt that it was.

Lily rose to her feet and walked to the office window, needed the distraction of the busy London scene outside, the throngs of people, the red double-decker buses and the snarl of traffic. *Her* office, she reminded herself as she sought to ground herself with a reminder of where she was now, the woman she was today a long way from that frightened child.

Lily Culpepper, founder and owner of Culpepper Housekeeping Services, a niche, prestigious company that recruited housekeepers and other private staff for global clients. She looked round her London office, thought of all her plans for expansion and reminded herself of how hard she'd worked to get here.

That was what was important. As for the hen break…damn it, she didn't want to go, but she would, even if sometimes she wondered why she didn't just walk away from the whole damn fiasco.

But walking away from Cynthia and Tom would mean walking away from her mother and, despite the complexities of their relationship, Lily couldn't do that. She didn't understand Maria, and knew Maria didn't understand her—they were chalk and cheese, and always had been, but Maria was her mum and the only real family Lily had.

So she'd stuck around, also determined not to give Cynthia the satisfaction of seeing how hurt she was. At the start she'd hung on to the humiliating hope that Tom would see that he'd got it wrong, see Cynthia for who she truly was. But that hadn't happened; instead, they'd announced their engagement, and pride had dictated Lily smile and congratulate them. Now that same pride decreed she would have to face the sun-soaked island.

Well, so be it; she wouldn't run scared, she'd show up and show them all how far she'd come—prove to them and herself that they no longer had any power over her. She'd suck it up, get through it. Because, however much she might wish it, no fairy godmother was going to turn up, wave a magic wand and say, *Lily, you shall not go on the hen break!* whilst the messages on her phone all turned to pumpkin emojis.

Because magic didn't exist, and neither did fairy godmothers or happy endings. She'd believed in all that once, had fought to believe it all her life, but no longer.

A knock on the door interrupted her reflections and she turned, a small frown on her face. Clients needed to buzz through from the foyer to be allowed in, plus she didn't have any appointments that day. Perhaps it was someone from one of the other offices.

'Come in.'

The door opened and a woman entered, not a woman Lily knew, though definitely one she recognised. A quick scan of her memory banks and the woman's identity was found—Lady Gemma Fairley-Godfrey, a woman in her sixties, incredibly wealthy, having inherited a family fortune. She'd never married, though she'd been linked with any number of celebrities, and was also known as a formidable fundraiser, renowned for her charity work.

She was also a former 'wild child' and supermodel who had recently adorned the cover of the world's most prestigious fashion magazine in an outfit that could at best be described as 'revealing'. A true role model in the art of ageing gracefully, and right now she looked pretty good.

Immaculately groomed, her ash-blonde hair was expertly dyed and styled to frame a classically beautiful face with high, slanted cheek-bones. Her widely spaced eyes were a clear emerald-green, adding a piquancy that the world's most renowned photographers had captured many times.

Whilst her beauty was undeniable, Lady Fairley-Godfrey had more than that. Like Lily's mother, she had an indefinable something—the 'it' factor or 'X factor' or whatever factor it was that gave beauty an additional twist, lifting it into the super-beauty category. Lily's mother had used it all her life to cajole, persuade and, in the end, ruthlessly win whichever hapless, rich male she targeted. Lily herself had inherited neither beauty nor any super-power herself; her genes presumably came from her dad's side, whoever he was. His identity a secret her mother refused to divulge.

But none of this mattered now, because Lady Fairley-Godfrey could be a prospective client and that could only add to the agency's prestige. It was well-known that only the best was good enough for this successful woman, known not to suffer fools gladly.

Lily stepped forward.

'Lily Culpepper?'

'Yes.' Lily held out a hand and the other woman shook it, a cool professional hand shake.

'Please sit down, Lady Fairley-Godfrey.'

'Thank you. And please call me Gemma. I am sorry to turn up without an appointment but I was in the area, saw your sign, remembered that you had been recommended to me and thought I'd drop in on the off chance.'

'Of course. Please sit down. How can I help?'

'I am planning a last-minute Valentine fundraiser for charity—a rehabilitation refuge that supports women and children in difficult situations, gives struggling mothers a chance to rebuild their life—perhaps saves a child from going into care. I plan to host a dinner dance for some very wealthy donors. My godson has offered his villa in Morocco, but it needs bringing up to scratch. I am planning on flying out myself to oversee things, but I need a housekeeper. Some guests will be staying, and I want to offer a five-star service.'

Lily thought rapidly. 'It's the end of January now,' she said thoughtfully. 'That's not a lot of time. But I am sure we can help. I'll need exact dates, then I can put together a shortlist of candidates for you to meet, or I can make a choice for you…'

Gemma shook her head, her green eyes holding a steely determination. 'No, you misunderstand. I want you to do it—personally.'

'Me? I'm flattered but I don't really take assignments on myself now, simply because...'

'You have a business to run. I understand that.' Gemma's voice was a touch impatient, that of a woman used to getting her own way. 'But nowadays you can do so much with technology. You could do a lot of that from Morocco, and surely you can delegate to someone here? It will only be for a week. I want the best. It's your company—I am assuming that is what you are.'

Lily's mind raced. Working for Gemma would gain Culpepper's a massive kudos boost, and oddly she didn't get the feeling Gemma was trying to push her around. It was more of a statement—she wanted the best person for the job and she had decided Lily was it. But in all honesty that wasn't Lily's prevailing thought right now—her prevailing thought was the realisation that, if she was working in Morocco, then she couldn't be on a sun-soaked island on a hen break.

And no one could question the validity of her excuse. No one would pass up the opportunity to work for Lady Fairley-Godfrey.

'I'll do it.'

Morocco, three days later

Darius Kingsleigh walked towards the villa, *his* villa, and looked at the sprawling dusk-pink terracotta walls embedded with arched latticed windows, walls that encased nine vast bedrooms, nine bathrooms, two enormous reception rooms, a dining room and a state-of-the-art kitchen. All set in an elegant mosaic courtyard enclosed by trellises. He'd purchased the villa a year ago entirely as a statement to himself, because he could. Just as he had purchased a sports car and apartments in both London and New York—with *his* money, money earned fair and square by him, from a company he'd set up himself.

A company that had nothing whatsoever to do with the Kingsleigh Hotel empire, founded over a hundred years ago, still family owned and now a global multi-billion enterprise run by his aunt and her children. Specifically not run by Darius himself, because his father, Enzo Kingsleigh, hadn't left him any shares in the business.

In point of fact, Enzo had left him nothing, not a proverbial dime. Instead, he had left his 'natural son' his 'best wishes'. An image of his father seemed to hover in the air, dark hair tinged with grey, larger than life, a man who'd denied himself nothing and had perhaps paid the price, collapsing from a massive unexpected heart attack at the age of sixty-five.

Grief, hurt, resentment, and guilt at that resentment all churned in a familiar twist in his gut, emotions that had roiled and darkened within him since Enzo's death three years ago.

Enough. Not now.

He'd moved on—moved on from Enzo, moved on from the whole Kingsleigh family. He'd made it in his own right and he damn well hoped that somehow Enzo knew that.

And then came the guilt again because, however reluctantly, however ungraciously, Enzo had accepted the truth of the DNA test and had accepted paternity and responsibility, taking Darius in. And for that he was grateful. That was why he had accepted the will, determined not to show his 'family' his true feelings. He'd left the plush, streamlined offices of the Kingsleigh lawyers and walked away. And he'd kept on walking, hadn't looked back for three years.

But soon the family drama would be exposed. He had received a courtesy call from the lawyers, informing him that probate should finally be granted in the next few weeks. Then the will would be open to public view. The whole world would know that Enzo Kingsleigh had disinherited his only son. Speculation would run rife.

Standing here now in the Moroccan sun, frustration twisted his gut. He could manage the fallout from the gossip sites. The issue was the impact on his company, the possibility of a shareholder upset, the question marks over his business prowess and his capability to run his business. The domino effect could be disastrous. Ironic that his father's opinion could matter beyond the grave.

But it could. The business world would wonder why Enzo had decided not to leave his son a single share in the Kingsleigh empire, had in fact elected to leave him nothing. It would ask if it was because Darius had proven himself to be a failure, whether he was nothing more than a playboy not to be trusted with the Kingsleigh legacy. Hurt seared again at the knowledge that Enzo hadn't trusted him, had never accepted him as a true Kingsleigh.

Darius closed his eyes, inhaling deeply. No matter; that could not be changed. But he would not let anything—speculation or gossip—impact his company. He would ride the storm. At least he had spent the past two years, since his disastrous liaison with Ruby AllStar, avoiding all publicity on a personal level, intent on ensuring all the public saw was Darius Kingsleigh, successful businessman, not a playboy.

Another deep breath and he collected his thoughts, focusing now on what lay ahead in the immediate future. He held back a sigh. In truth he did not have time for this; he should be at work, but he hadn't been able to refuse his godmother's request.

Their earlier conversation flitted through his mind.

'Darius, I need a favour.'

There'd been no small talk and no build-up, no general enquiries as to his well-being, so Darius had known his godmother's need was real. Her image on the computer screen had held unwonted signs of strain.

'Go ahead.'

'I'm due to be in Morocco later today.'

He'd nodded. 'Yup, to get the villa ready for your fundraiser. You got the keys, right?'

'Yes, I have the keys, but there's a problem. I'm needed elsewhere.'

She hadn't elaborated and Darius hadn't asked. His godmother had so many people and causes that there was always someone some-where who needed her. He'd been one of those people himself.

'OK. What do I need to do…?'

The answer to that question had been a concise set of instructions. Now, twenty hours later, here he was.

He crossed the tiled courtyard, walked up the balustraded stairs towards the imposing arched door and frowned when he saw it was slightly ajar. Presumably the woman he was here to meet, Lily Culpepper, had already gone in, but why would she have left the door open? He entered, stood for a moment in the wide mosaic hallway, then heard a noise from the room to his right and moved towards it—just as a woman purposefully walked out, a woman with keys in hand and a cobweb in her dark-brown hair. He tried to sidestep but too late; the inevitable collision happened and he instinctively reached out to steady them both, his hands on her arms as they both stared at each other.

Arrest took him completely by surprise. There was a jolt of awareness, a spark, a sense of physical connection that shocked him into immobility. He saw a reciprocal realisation in a pair of wide, dark-blue eyes. Then he saw recognition dawn; she'd worked out who he was and her lips tightened in what was surely disapproval. Lips that, despite himself, he lingered on for a fraction of a second too long before stepping back.

'You must be Lily Culpepper,' he said, studying her properly now, trying to work out what had triggered the reaction. Dark-brown hair fell straight to her shoulders; her face was oval, with a determined chin; her best feature was her eyes, dark-blue and fringed with long, dark lashes. Her nose was a trifle long, giving her face character, and her mouth was generous.

She nodded. 'And you are Darius Kingsleigh.' Her voice was neutral but there was a fleeting look of judgment in her eyes and for some reason it caught him on the raw. He'd had more than enough judgment in his lifetime.

'Yes. I'm Gemma's godson. I assume you're expecting me and that's why the door was open? Just as a note, I expect my staff to be security conscious. I'd prefer my villa not to be ransacked.'

Even as he said the words he wondered what the hell he was doing; he'd come across as a pompous jackass, his tone condescending, all based on a possible misinterpretation of her expression.

Before he could attempt to retrieve the situation, anger flashed across her eyes. 'Last I looked, I am not *your* staff. My company has been hired by Lady Fairley-Godfrey, and I am contracted to her. Furthermore, I'm not sure when you last visited *your* villa, or how you left it, but right now the lock is broken.'

Ah. Now he came to think of it, when he'd bought it a year ago the estate agent had said something about there being a knack to the lock. 'It took me fifteen minutes to manage to open the door and get in. I then decided to leave it open as I didn't want to lock myself in until I knew there was another way out. I left it unsecured for about two minutes. But by all means, now you are here, feel free to lock the door. I will wait for Gemma outside—she is due here any minute.'

She stepped forward, keys held out, and on automatic he reached out to take them, his fingers inadvertently brushing hers—and there it was again, an instantaneous reaction, the type that in a film would warrant little cartoon blue sparks on the screen. They both snatched their hands back and the keys fell to the ground with a clatter.

With a muttered exclamation of annoyance, she dived to get them just as he squatted down to do the same. Now they were both on the floor, practically face to face, so close he could see the smatter of freckles on the bridge of her nose, observe exactly how long her eyelashes were, smell the light floral scent she wore, and watch the sunlight coming through the crack in the door highlight the gloss of her hair.

And she was as mesmerised as he, her blue eyes darkening, her lips slightly parting, and somehow, instead of moving backwards, instead of reaching for the keys, they were both moving slightly closer to each other. For a crazy second he hoped, wished, that she would kiss him…and then the door creaked, the sound breaking the spell, and she muttered something that sounded suspiciously like, 'Idiot,' and scrambled to her feet.

Picking up the keys, he followed suit and for a moment they stood in silence. He knew he should say something, knew the longer the silence stretched the more awkward this was all becoming, but he couldn't think of anything to say. What had happened to Darius Kingsleigh, suave dater of celebrities? He'd eschewed relationships for two years, but he'd have thought some vestige of flair would have remained.

In the end it was Lily who tucked a tendril of hair behind her ear and took a step towards the door.

'I'll wait outside for Gemma.'

'No, there's no point. Gemma isn't coming.'

'Of course she is coming—her fundraiser is in less than a week and she is coming here to organise it.'

Darius took a deep breath. 'That's what I'm

here to do. Gemma can't make it; she is needed elsewhere. She'll be back for the actual event, but in the meantime I'm her deputy, and she has asked if you and I can get the villa ready and plan the event.'

She took a step backwards, and then, her voice slightly strangled, she said, 'You and me?'

The 'you' was said with both disbelief and a definite hint of horror, something he empathised with. In their short acquaintance, Lily Culpepper had already completely unsettled him, and the situation was beginning to grate on his already somewhat frayed nerves.

'Yes. Is that a problem?'

CHAPTER TWO

YES—IT WAS most definitely a bloody problem, with a capital P, for multiple reasons. Lily inhaled deeply, took a calming breath and wondered how on earth she'd lost such spectacular control of events.

One of her biggest strengths was her ability to remain cool and unflappable at all times— an ability she'd learnt and cultivated over the years from the moment she'd realised that she was different from other children because her mother was different. Then had honed when she'd realised the best way to face down the bullying was not to show emotion, to make them think she didn't care.

It was a trait that had stood her in good stead through the horror of Cynthia and Tom's wedding preparations, and she'd believed it to be an ingrained part of her. Yet in an instant Darius Kingsleigh had undermined all of that. That initial collision had triggered a reaction that even now she did not want to believe.

No way—*surely* no way—could she be attracted to this man. He was a man who had graced any number of celebrity magazines over the years, with any number of different women. A man often said to be a carbon copy of his father—Enzo Kingsleigh had been notorious for his party lifestyle and his son had followed suit. They both embodied everything Lily despised: people who used looks and wealth to get what they wanted. Worse than that, every affair had been brief, and no doubt Darius left broken hearts in his wake.

She could still recall his much-publicised break from the popular singer-songwriter Ruby AllStar and her accusation that he'd strung her along, promising commitment. So he might have looks, but she knew those looks were not backed up by the things Lily believed to be important—integrity, kindness, a work ethic where a person worked for what they got and didn't have it handed it to them on a silver platter.

Yet his looks were playing havoc with her hormones, which was all wrong. Lily told herself she was overreacting. She hadn't known his identity when she'd first reacted and her hormones simply hadn't caught up with events.

Regardless, the most important thing was to get everything onto a professional footing. She'd been rude to her client's godson, not a good move, and an even worse move now that it turned out he was acting for the client.

She took a deep breath and tugged her jacket down in a decisive movement, looking across at Darius and seeing that his earlier anger seemed to have gone. Instead, there was a hint of amusement in his eyes. 'Did you know you have a very expressive face?' he asked.

Great. Marvellous.

'No,' she said repressively. 'I didn't know that because usually I don't.'

'Well, today you do, and I have a feeling you do have a problem with the idea of working with me—that you know what the problem is but you are trying to remind yourself to be professional and rise above it.' Now he smiled. 'How am I doing?'

Lily really wished he hadn't smiled, because the smile was doing something strange to her. It was a smile that reached his eyes, crinkled them ever so lightly and sparked them with humour and an invitation to smile back. She could feel her treacherous, expressive face wanted to do just that.

Not happening. Because now incipient panic

was trickling in alongside a sense of confusion. She couldn't remember the last time anyone had read her so easily, couldn't really remember a time when anyone had been interested enough in her reactions to read them at all. And she didn't like it. With a supreme effort, she kept her face neutral. 'The problem isn't personal,' she said. 'I prefer to work alone or with a colleague of my own choosing.'

'You would have been working with my godmother.'

'That's different.'

'Why?'

Good question. 'Your godmother was the original client. She is the one I agreed to work for. And now that job spec has changed.'

'Is it about money? Gemma said she'll pay you more.'

'It's not about money.'

'You're worried you won't be able to do the new job?'

'No!' She narrowed her eyes. *Damn it.* Darius was toying with her and she could see where this was headed.

'Then it *must* be me,' he said. 'If I had been the original client, would you have refused the job?' His voice was polite, gentle even, but it was underlaid with an edge of steel. An edge that reminded Lily that, as well as being a party-loving serial dater, Darius was also an incredibly successful businessman—founder and CEO of a company that turned over billions, a company that had achieved runaway global success in the past two-and-a-half years.

'That is a hypothetical scenario,' she said.

'Yup. So let's hypothesise.'

'There is no point.'

'There is every point. Because right now I am effectively the client, so we have a choice to make: whether we can work together or not, as Gemma has requested.'

Unfortunately... 'You're right.' Could she work with this man? *Really, Lily?* Was she even asking the question, or suggesting that she couldn't work with him because she couldn't control her hormones? The sheer shallowness of the idea added an edge to her annoyance. As for personal feelings, she might not like or approve of his lifestyle, but as a professional surely she could work with him on a charity fundraiser?

'If we can't, we risk not getting the job done in time, and that wouldn't be fair to Gemma or the charity,' he pointed out. 'So I have an idea. It's nearly eight o'clock and I'm hungry. How about we go and have dinner whilst we discuss the best way forward? Gemma has given me plenty of information about what she wants us to do. Let's go and see if it's viable. If not, I'll pay you for your time so far and figure out what to do next.'

There was that edge again and Lily forced herself not to glare at him as determination solidified within her. No way was she losing this job; she was good at what she did and she was not going to let some ridiculous attraction get in the way. She was a consummate professional and now was the time to prove it. She would not let this man's looks affect her—it would be despicable. Would be almost a validation of her mother's way of life—the way she'd used her beauty as currency without caring a damn for the repercussions it had brought to so many lives, including Lily's own.

It had been enough to make her believe with all her heart that looks shouldn't matter, to make her vow always to judge people by their character. Which made it all the more mortifying to find her errant hormones betraying every one of her principles and reacting as they had to Darius Kingsleigh.

But, then again—and the thought stopped her in her tracks—he'd looked pretty poleaxed too. She shook her head. She must have imagined it, wishful thinking on her hormones' part. Darius dated beautiful celebrities, not an average-looking businesswoman whose company turned over a fraction of his wealth.

Lily had no illusions about her looks. Not since the moment her five-year-old self first overheard a conversation between two of the mothers at school.

'Isn't it odd, a beautiful woman like Maria produced such a plain little girl?'

'Maybe she's adopted.'

It had been a conversation she'd encountered countless times since, and she'd long since decided simply to accept her looks and focus on making something of her life through her achievements.

'Dinner is fine,' she said, even as instinct told her dinner sounded all wrong. 'I'd picked out a local restaurant to go to with good reviews. Does that sound OK?' She braced herself for a refusal: perhaps a small local eatery wouldn't be good enough for him.

'Works for me,' he said.

Actually, why wouldn't it? This wasn't a date; plus he'd probably be embarrassed to be spotted or snapped with someone as ordinary as her. He was studying her expression now, a slight frown on his face, as if he was trying to read her thoughts, and she kept her expression strictly neutral—there'd be no more giveaway expressions.

'Then let's go,' she said.

Darius nodded, even as he wondered why he'd extended a dinner invitation. Why he hadn't simply fired her on the spot. He was pretty sure that was what Enzo would have done.

Hell, he was through with doing what Enzo had done. He'd spent twenty years doing that, desperate to prove himself worthy of being Enzo's son. To show Enzo, show the world, that he possessed the Kingsleigh gene. He'd done what his father had, had lived his father's lifestyle, had partied, womanised and worked for the Kingsleigh empire, trying everything to show Enzo he was his true son, his blood.

All to no avail; the taste of failure was bitter on his tongue even now, three years after Enzo's death. Now it was too late, too late to win his father's love or recognition.

Perhaps it had always been too late. His father had done his duty, but love had been a step too far, and maybe that fault had lain with Darius, not Enzo. Now all he could do was focus on succeeding in his own right, on his own terms, on his own. Because that was how he liked it.

On his own, there was nothing to prove to

anyone. No worry that one day the person he trusted to be there would leave without warning—the way his mother had gone. She might not have been the best mother in the world, but she'd been all he had, and he'd loved her. He'd believed she'd loved him, and his eight-year-old self had been devastated when she'd gone, even if he had the bleak knowledge and shame that he'd brought it on himself.

He took a deep breath, eyed Lily Culpepper and wondered whether it might not be better to pay her off and do this on his own. There'd be no one to answer to and, even better, no unsettling attraction to complicate things. He didn't even understand why he was attracted to her. He was pretty sure she didn't even like him, which was annoying him far more than it should. Why should he give a damn about her opinion?

'Let's go,' he agreed. With any luck, by the end of dinner she'd decide she couldn't work with him anyway.

They left the house and he pulled the door, having spent a few minutes figuring out the mechanism, before he'd managed to pull it shut. He took one last look at his statement purchase, wondering if he'd bought it in an unconscious tribute to his father—the purchase of a villa on a whim the final following of his footsteps.

Though Enzo would have filled it with guests and thrown lavish parties. Darius had bought it and then left it; he could barely recall the interior. At least now it would be put to good use.

He glanced at his companion, appreciating the fact that Lily seemed content to walk in silence; there was no need for small talk as they made their way along the pavements, where the owners of small shops were putting up their shutters, until they came to a paved square full of cafés.

Lily looked down at her phone and then pointed. 'That's the one.'

Darius looked at the busy restaurant, the tiled paved outside area filled with tables interspersed with cleverly placed verdant plants in terracotta pots. 'Good choice,' he said. 'I've eaten here before. Just the once, but I do remember the food is outstanding.'

They entered the restaurant, where rows of wooden tables covered in woven rattan mats were filled with people eating and talking, the clatter of cutlery, the buzz of conversation and an array of tantalising smells all combined. Lily glanced round and bit her lip. 'It's pretty busy. I should have booked.'

Before he could answer, a woman headed towards them. 'You've come back,' she said, and smiled.

Darius blinked and wound his mind back to a year ago, recalled enjoying the meal, appreciating the quiet corner table and the excellent food. But he was pretty sure he'd never seen this woman.

He settled for, 'Yes,' and turned as the woman was joined by a man and an older lady, one he did recognise. 'You were here when I was here last,' he said and the woman nodded.

'That was me,' she said.

The man stepped forward, held out his hand. 'I am Jamal. I own the restaurant, and I'm also the chef. This is my wife, Natalia, and this is my mother. It was my mother who took a picture of you last year.'

Darius still wasn't sure where this was going.

'We had just opened and Mama put the picture in the local paper and on our website. It showed you with an empty plate in front of you, and we got lots of customers. Then we heard that you had bought the villa and we have been hoping you would come in.' Jamal's smile was apologetic. 'Mama put the picture up without telling me,' he explained. 'We know we maybe should have asked permission and…'

'We did take it all down very soon.'

It seemed clear that Jamal and Natalia were concerned, apprehensive, even. It was the sort of thing that his family would have got all strange about; they would have talked about permissions and copyrights, but not as far as Darius was concerned. 'I am pretty sure it was the excellence of your food that brought the customers in.' He smiled reassuringly. 'But, if my picture helped in any way, I am glad.'

'Thank you.' The relief was palpable as Jamal beamed at him. 'Now, come be seated. This dinner is on the house and we promise it will be one you remember.'

Natalia smiled. 'And this time no photos, we promise. We have a table all ready for you both, in a small private room. My sister has been getting it ready whilst we have been talking. Come.'

'Thank you.' It was the first time Lily had spoken, but he had been aware of her quiet presence beside him, sensing her scrutiny, and now he saw her give him a small glance of surprise. Then she turned to Natalia; soon the two women were chatting, and Darius tried not to notice the swish and gloss of Lily's brown hair or watch the grace and elegance with which she walked.

Until they arrived at the table and Lily came to a sudden halt, breaking off mid-sentence, and as he took in the scene Darius understood why.

CHAPTER THREE

LILY STARED AT the table, above which floated a massive heart-shaped helium balloon inscribed with 'Be My Valentine'. On the table there was an array of finger food arranged on heart-shaped silver plates with gleaming cutlery, a snow-white linen table cloth and red napkins with a border of…hearts…and two cocktails with heart flags resting over the rims, a scattering of rose petals.

Clearly, in their desire to create a memorable occasion, the owners had grasped entirely the wrong end of the stick and assumed this was a date. Darius was a serial dater, he was known to own the villa round the corner and had turned up in the evening with a woman—what else would they assume?

Natalia beamed at her, clearly assuming Lily's silence indicated surprised appreciation. 'I hope you like it. We will be doing a Valentine special and I had already purchased the stock. Jamal is going to prepare the Valentine menu for you too.'

It was time to set the situation straight. Lily opened her mouth to explain this was strictly business...and then she saw the expression on Darius's face: a dismay even greater than her own etched his handsome features and a sudden anger pinged inside her. Of course he was mortified; no doubt the thought of anyone thinking he would lower his standards to date someone like Lily, let alone be her valentine, horrified him.

It was reminiscent of Tom's dismay two years ago, on Valentine's Day. Memories streamed her mind of the dinner she'd prepared, every ingredient purchased with love; the table laid, complete with a heart-shaped helium balloon of her own. The whole evening was supposed to have heralded the start of the rest of her life, with the man she loved.

Instead, it had been the scene of her humiliation and rejection and all she'd been left with after Tom's shame-faced departure was the congealed food and the sauce that had bubbled away, evaporating just as all her hopes and dreams had, leaving nothing but a burnt layer on the pan and the bitter ashes of a future that was never to be.

The memory was so clear, so painful, and anger tightened inside her, transmuted into a raw sear of hurt, of fury at Darius's expression. She turned to Natalia. 'This is beautiful, and Darius and I so appreciate this early chance to celebrate Valentine's. It feels like the whole of this month should be about celebrating romance.'

Even as she spoke her brain began to catch up with her mouth. What was she doing? She was supposed to be winning over Darius Kingsleigh with her professionalism and here she was, pretending to be his date. He'd think she was a fruit loop. She *was* a fruit loop and he was no doubt about to expose her as exactly that.

Instead, a wide smile on his face, he stepped forward so he was stood next to her and she gave a small, involuntary gasp. 'Thank you—this is an unanticipated pleasure.'

'Then sit down, enjoy the champagne cocktail, make a start on the canapés and I will bring the main course when it is ready.'

Once Natalia was gone, Darius put down his glass with a *thunk*. 'Mind telling me what all that was about?'

Lily took a small defiant sip of her cocktail and jutted out her chin. No way was she going to explain the truth. 'I thought it was a shame to rain on their parade. They'd gone to so much trouble; there didn't seem to be any harm in going along with it.'

His stare intensified, his grey eyes hard and unreadable, though she could sense anger behind the set of his lips.

'No harm?' he repeated. 'Have you considered what will happen if Jamal or Natalia or a member of staff mention to someone that we were here, or if another diner pops their head round the door by mistake?'

'Oh.' This was Darius Kingsleigh, a member of the Kingsleigh family, loved by the media for providing them with scandals and stories galore. A single picture of Darius had launched the restaurant. Darius having a romantic dinner with a woman would be seen as an event in its own right in the eyes of the gossip sites. Lily closed her eyes and wished really hard that she could rewind time, rewrite the past hour to how it should have been. But she couldn't.

'OK. Obviously, I wasn't thinking straight.' *Or at all.* Incipient panic touched her—how could she have been so unprofessional? She couldn't blame Darius for questioning her ability to do the job. Why had she even cared what Darius thought about her on a personal level?

'And I apologise. I acted on instinct. I can go and speak to Natalia and clear it up now.'

There was a silence and then he shook his head. 'Apology accepted, and no need. I think it will cause more questions than it will solve— no smoke without fire, et cetera. That's why I went along with it. Hopefully there'll be no damage. I don't think anyone noticed us when we came in and they have already promised no photographs.' He gestured at the plates. 'I think the best thing to do will be to have dinner as planned and hope we stay under the radar.'

Lily nodded, looking at the plates that adorned the table. They held plump, luscious olives, both green and a deep dark brown; delicious-looking fava beans marinated in spices and herbs; various triangular, square and rectangle pastries and an array of different condiments.

Darius pushed a plate of the pastries towards her and pointed at a bright-red paste. 'I remember from last time how incredible these pastry things are, especially dipped in the harissa sauce.'

Lily pushed down the usual sense of discomfort at eating food recommended by other people, people she didn't know or didn't trust. As always, she told herself she was being irrationally paranoid. This was food prepared by a professional chef—of course it would be fine.

'The sauce is tangy, but it's not too hot.'

Wrong thing to say, though there was no way Darius could know that. But his words triggered another throwback memory. She was back at the boarding school that her mother and stepfather had also sent her stepsisters to, so they could 'bond'.

In truth Maria had wanted to cement her new marriage and ensure she thoroughly enslaved her husband so that he didn't regret signing a pre-nup agreement that his lawyer had visibly blanched at and had advised heavily against.

So she'd come up with the boarding school idea, ignoring Lily's pleas not to send her. 'You need to toughen up. Make yourself popular and you'll be fine.'

Not advice Lily had been able to figure out, but her stepsisters had and, once they'd achieved popularity, they had made bullying Lily into their favourite group sport.

One of the games had been food-orientated; they'd doctored Lily's food with salt or spices. And then had been the worst of all—a group had surrounded her and one of the girls, one Lily had always thought was nicer than the rest, had stepped forward.

'Here,' she'd said, holding out a plate with brownies on it. 'We wanted to say sorry. It's a peace offering. Try it.'

Lily had looked round, seen no sign of either stepsister and had allowed herself to let hope trump common sense. She had taken one and bitten into it… She could still recall the pain as she'd realised it had been doctored with chilli powder. Her mouth had been set on fire, lips burning, throat scorched, eyes and nose running to the mocking laughter of the girls.

'Earth to Lily.' She blinked now and saw Darius looking at her, a small frown furrowing his brow. 'You OK?'

'Yes. Of course.' She had to get a grip. 'This does look incredible,' she added, trying to inject enthusiasm into her tone.

'I think you'll like it. From what I remember—' he pointed as he spoke '—the triangular pastries are potato-filled and the tubes are beef-filled. As for the harissa, just to be on the safe side, I'll test it first in case Jamal has changed the recipe and it's ridiculously hot.'

It was almost as if he had read her mind but she told herself that simply wasn't possible. For anyone, but particularly not a man like Darius, who judged the worth of his dinner companions by their looks and status. And yet…his words had reassured her, had calmed the irrational jitters.

He picked up a pastry and dipped it in the harissa sauce. Somehow the movement mesmerised her; the shape of his bare forearm, the strength of his wrist and the breadth of his fingers all combined to send a sudden shot of liquid desire through her veins.

'Just as good as I remember, and not too hot, I promise.' The depth of his voice shivered over her skin and she couldn't help it; she smiled and, after a moment, he smiled back with a toe-curling smile. 'The exact right level of heat and spice.'

Oh, God, was he flirting with her? Did she want him to flirt with her? Lily blinked hard, the questions wiping the smile straight off her face. This was the sort of thing Darius probably did on automatic, using charm, banter and his looks to lure women in. No way would it work on her; no way would she *let* it work on her.

She picked up a pastry, dipped it in the sauce and took a bite, relishing the crunch of the pastry, the contrast with the softness of the potato spiced with turmeric, the whole thing perfectly complemented by the tang of chilli in the harissa. 'Yup. This is really good. You were right—the food is outstanding. Maybe I can take inspiration from Jamal's menu for the dinner for the fundraiser. If we decide that I am going ahead with the job.'

Perhaps there was a smidge of relief in his eyes as he nodded. 'Time to talk business,' he agreed.

It really was, Darius reflected as he picked up another pastry, this time filled with cumin-laced beef. This whole meeting was not panning out as he'd expected, his head dizzied by the twists and turns. He still wasn't sure he bought Lily's explanation for why she'd decided to pretend this was a date but that wasn't the biggest issue.

The problem was this *felt* like a date, with a level of attraction that flared and hummed under its own control. And he didn't like that; he needed to bring this *business* meeting under his control, establish a professional footing.

'How about we start with you telling me what Gemma hired you to do, I'll then explain how that has changed and we can work out the best way forward?'

'That sounds like a plan.' She marshalled her thoughts and he couldn't help but notice the serious look in her dark-blue eyes, the small crease of concentration as she tucked a tendril of brown hair behind her ear.

'My job was to get the villa up to five-star luxury standard and then act as housekeeper, with a capital H, for all the guests who will be staying in the villa. Ensure they are supplied with everything they need, from towels, to breakfast, to picnic hampers.'

He nodded. 'As you know, the plan is to have a Valentine-themed dinner for the six couples who will be staying in the villa. After that another twenty couples will arrive for dancing, and entertainment. That now all needs to be organised.'

'So we need caterers, a menu, a band and to figure out the entertainment. Something different—your godmother is known for the uniqueness of her events.'

Darius glanced at her. 'Do you also deal with event planning?'

'No, but housekeepers tend to get involved in all sorts of social functions. I'm confident I can help with the organisational side of things.'

'What about the impact of the increased workload? Gemma mentioned you own your business.'

'I do.' Pride crossed her face, a pride he empathised with. 'I can manage—this will be a lot of work, but in a short period of time it won't be a problem. I wouldn't take it on if I thought it would impact either the fundraiser or my existing clients.'

There was sincerity and professional pride in her voice and he nodded. 'I understand why Gemma employed you—she only employs the best.'

'Thank you,' she said and there it was again— the same smile that had blindsided him earlier, a smile that lit up her face and chased away the slight reserve it held in repose, a wariness that he wasn't sure was directed at the world or just him personally.

And now his breath caught in his throat. The candlelight lit her face, showing the small smatter of freckles on the slant of her cheekbone and emphasising the character of her face and the sparkle in the blue eyes fringed by those impossibly long lashes. Of their own volition, her eyes fell to his lips and he realised that she seemed as transfixed as he was, her eyes scanning his face.

Until her phone rang out, breaking the spell as she looked away to grab it. 'Sorry. I should have switched it off or at least put it on silent.' She glanced down and quickly declined the call. Within seconds it shrilled out again, and now she pressed another button which cut the sound, though he could still hear it vibrating.

'Why don't you take it?' he asked as the door opened. 'It looks like they are bringing in the next course, so you'll have a few minutes.'

'In that case, I will. I'll be back in two minutes, give or take.' Turning, she smiled at Natalia. 'Thank you. That was all amazing so far.'

Darius forced himself not to watch her walk to the door and refused to ogle the natural grace and sway of her body. But, damn it, it was hard and he could see Natalia suppress a small smile when he turned to look at her; he realised he'd added to the whole illusory 'date' scenario.

Natalia continued to beam at him. 'Jamal asked me to explain the thinking behind the dinner.'

She started to speak and Darius resisted a groan.

CHAPTER FOUR

Lily slipped into the bathroom and locked the door, picking up her still ringing phone.

'Hi, Mum. I am sorry, but this isn't a great time. I'm in a meeting.'

'At this time of night?' There was a sigh down the phone. 'You should be out having fun.'

'This is my idea of fun.'

'Is your meeting with Lady Fairley-Godfrey? That would at least be something.'

Lily weighed up her options, unsure what her mother would do if she told her she was having dinner with Darius Kingsleigh—combust, no doubt. So she settled for, 'It's a representative, and he is waiting at the table, so I'd better get back.'

'A representative? A man? Dinner? What are you wearing? Have you got make-up on? Is he rich?'

'I'm wearing black trousers and a top—it's a professional meeting,' Lily said repressively.

'I don't understand you and why you won't make more of yourself and opportunities like this.'

'Mum, we've been here before.'

So many times; an all too familiar frustration rolled through her. For her whole life, Lily had resisted her mother's attempts to make her follow in her footsteps, to emulate her philosophy. Maria had no objection as such to her daughter wanting a job, but she thought securing a wealthy man was way more important. 'And actually a lot more lucrative,' as she was fond of pointing out.

But Lily didn't get it, or understand why her mother didn't care about the emotional fallout her lifestyle led to. As a child, Lily had been shunted from one friend to another to keep her out of the way so her mother could give her undivided attention to her 'lucrative' man, who also happened to be married.

Then her mother had moved on to target another married man, only this time she'd upped the ante, had won him away from his wife and married him herself, thus securing a lifetime income. Maria had seen this as a triumph, seeming oblivious to the fact it had broken up a home and gained Lily two stepsisters who loathed her, and spent years tormenting her—sufficient that Lily's school life had been a living hell that she'd emerged from with no qualifications.

The result being that Lily had vowed that she would never follow in her mother's footsteps and would instead forge a real career and rely on herself for money.

Lily tuned back in to the conversation. 'Mum, I really do have to go. Why were you calling?'

'I wanted to know whether there is any way you can go to the hen event—Cynthia is very put out that you have pulled out. She thinks you should be prioritising family.'

'I can't leave this job,' Lily said firmly. She hung up, now doubly determined to close this deal. She needed this job. Professional pride aside, if she ended up on a plane home in a few days' time she would be on another plane to the sun-soaked island, pushed aboard by her mother.

The thought galvanised her into action, though it couldn't stop the *whoomph* of reaction as she approached the table and saw Darius: the dark, unruly, mid length hair; the face that was etched with a craggy strength; the breadth of his shoulder, the swell of muscle. The whole god damned package.

Enough.

Reaching the table, she sat down and looked at the spread of food on the table. 'This looks good.'

'It's a Valentine's special,' he said, a rueful tilt to his lips. 'Natalia explained it all. Jamal has put a lot of thought into it.'

'That's brilliant.' And a chance to show him that all she was thinking about was the job, *not* the tilt to his lips *or* the fine laughter lines around his eyes. 'Maybe we can use his ideas as inspiration for the fundraiser meal.'

'I'm not sure that would work.'

'Why not?' She tilted out her chin.

'Because I'm assuming our fundraiser theme is the soppy type of romance.' His voice held a hint of amusement that was reflected in his eyes, with an invitation to share the amusement that somehow warmed her, threatening to send her newly found resolve out of the window. 'This meal is more… Well, to quote Jamal, "it's saucy and steamy".'

'Oh.' *Saucy and steamy.* Heaven help her, it should sound cringe-worthy, but when Darius said it, it didn't. Instead the words sent a tingle through her whole body.

'Yup. I did promise to relay the whole spiel to you—Natalia wants our opinion as a couple, would like feedback at the end of the meal.'

'Oh.' *Great.* 'Go ahead.' She tried to keep her voice impersonal, as if this was simply a factual instruction.

'Here goes. Jamal suggests we start with this dish.' His voice was deep, his eyes still holding hers and, despite herself, she could feel a hum of awareness.

'Why?'

'Because it's spicy and sweet. A perfect blend—enough heat to keep things simmering and create a build-up.'

'Got it.' Her voice was a touch breathless as she watched him point to the next dish, and then his gaze was back on her, and she could see the grey eyes darken, was sure they held a promise, an invitation.

'Then he recommends we move onto this one, which packs more chillies—enough to cause a rush of heat.'

Lily forced herself to remain still, not to wriggle in her seat. She knew she had to say something, though the words that came out weren't what she'd intended.

'So all we need now,' she said, deadpan, 'is the perfect dessert that we can share for the perfect finish—the climax to the meal.'

She met his gaze full on and saw the grey eyes go molten. 'I can see you've got the hang of

Jamal's thinking,' he said. Now he smiled, and this time she really couldn't stop her answering smile.

The job, remember the job. That was the focus here; she couldn't afford to get distracted by the lure of his smile, or how would she be able to do this job to the best of her ability? Unless…

'I've had an idea,' she said.

'Go ahead.'

'I'm assuming you weren't expecting to be involved in organising the fundraiser?'

'No, I wasn't.'

'I'm also assuming you are a busy man.' Lily knew that he ran a company that she assumed was an offshoot of the Kingsleigh empire, one that he'd taken to global success over the past two-and-a-half years.

'Correct.'

'Then would you prefer Culpepper's to organise the event? You could go back home and I could provide you with a daily update—keep you posted on how everything is going. What do you think?' Surely he would jump at the chance to go back to his normal life?

'No,' he said. 'I appreciate the offer, but no.'

Lily stared at him; she'd been so sure he'd agree. 'Are you sure? I am perfectly capable.'

'I'm sure you are,' he said easily. 'But that isn't the point. My godmother asked me to do this, I agreed and I intend to honour that agreement. I had already agreed to provide the villa and undertake the expenses involved as my donation. If she needs my time as well, then I will give it. Whilst I am sure you would get the job done, for me it is more than a job, it's personal. I owe my godmother a lot—she has asked for my help and I want to give it.'

Damn it; he'd wrong-footed her and Lily could tell he was being sincere. And she couldn't help but respect him for it. It was easy for a man as rich as Darius to give money; it wasn't so easy to commit time and inconvenience. 'I understand,' she said. 'In that case...'

'In that case I suggest we do this together, as long as you are happy to work with me rather than Gemma.'

'Happy' was pushing it, yet to her surprise anticipation fluttered through her alongside a determination to do the very best job she could. 'I'm in.'

'Then we have a deal.' He held out his hand and without thinking she put hers in it, knowing the second his hand enclosed hers that it was a mistake. She did not believe in magic, instant sparks or connections. She quite simply didn't.

But his touch was doing *something* to her, sending a volt, a buzz of heat straight to her veins, and had taken the earlier awareness up a notch or three. This heat had nothing to do with sauce or spice; a shimmer of sparks seemed to have enmeshed them. Her hand was still in his and the sense of his skin on hers felt right, cool, strong and sending her a message way beyond sealing a deal.

She could sense herself leaning forward, and could see he was doing the same. Her brain seemed to have turned to mush, her entire being focused on the sensations rushing through her. Then the door opened and there was the sound of a throat clearing.

She dropped his hand, slamming back in her seat, and turned to see Jamal. Knew it was too late, that the restaurant owner had seen it all; knew too that her face was flushed and that she still looked dazed.

Jamal's face was apologetic but urgent. 'I am sorry to interrupt, but one of the diners has discovered that you are here having dinner in here. I think she is now trying to get access to the room. I wasn't sure if you minded?'

Lily saw annoyance flash across Darius's face, before he smiled. 'Thank you for the heads up. It's not your fault at all. Lily and I would rather avoid publicity, so if it's OK with you we'll slip out of a back exit. And can I just say, dinner was superb.'

'Thank you, and of course.' Jamal nodded. 'If you like, Natalia can give you a lift, rather than calling a taxi—for extra discretion.'

'That is very kind of you,' Lily said. 'And Darius is right—the dinner was superb. You will make a lot of Valentine diners very happy.'

CHAPTER FIVE

Darius noted that Lily elected to go in the passenger seat next to Natalia. 'You aren't a taxi,' she'd pointed out when Natalia had said they should both go in the back. He wondered if her motivation was based solely on common courtesy or whether she didn't want to risk the proximity to him.

Either way it was a good call. Proximity was definitely a bad idea; he could still feel Lily's hand in his. Her slender fingers seemed to have branded him, scorching him with a heat that had transcended all other thoughts and all common sense.

There was no point in denying the attraction—the moment of insanity when he would have acted on it and kissed Lily. What was wrong with him? He had no idea what her stance on relationships was, had set no ground rules. He had never once let attraction trump the need for rules, and never been tempted to kiss anyone without making sure those rules were in place.

Darius had always known the importance of relationship rules because he'd always known he didn't understand how relationships worked. He didn't understand how to win love, knew he didn't have the capacity to navigate a long-term relationship. Hell, he hadn't even known how to win his own parents' love.

So it seemed to him the best, the only, way for him to have a relationship was to set rules and boundaries that he *could* understand. To make sure there was no opportunity for love, no chance or expectation of it. It was always clear from the outset that any relationship could only be short term, because that was what he was capable of. That way, no one could get hurt.

Yet with Lily he'd have kissed her without a rule or boundary in place and that didn't make sense. And Darius didn't like things that didn't make sense, so the attraction needed to go.

He became aware of something nagging at his subconscious, figured out what it was as the little car slowed down to allow some pedestrians to cross the road. He turned his head to try and work out if his hunch was correct: that someone was following them.

Hard to tell—he might be overreacting but

experience told him there was every chance he wasn't. Not when he knew the fascination the press had with the Kingsleigh family. Perhaps it was the sheer extent of their wealth, and the level of scandals they had generated over time—something Enzo had been particularly good at. He'd lived hard, partied wildly and grabbed headlines. Had been an erratic presence in the boardroom but, whilst he'd had flashes of business acumen that had justified his place, it was his sister Rita Kingsleigh who held sway at the helm of the Kingsleigh empire.

Rita had groomed her three children to be the Kingsleigh heirs. Unlike Darius, they had all been fast tracked to the boardroom automatically, although all three seemed to have inherited the Kingsleigh love of partying, and were a delight to the press in their own right.

As Darius himself had been: from his late teens to early twenties, Darius had tried to follow in Enzo's footsteps and prove he was his father's son. He had dated celebrities, partied and played to the camera in ways designed to echo his father's exploits. So, whilst he'd avoided any scandal in the past two years, after the extensive coverage of his break-up with Ruby AllStar—hadn't dated anyone and had focused solely on his business—he knew the press would relish any story about him all the more.

And now was not the time. The press would have a bonanza of a story in the near future once Enzo's will was made public. When that broke Darius knew he would need to prove to the world that he was a true businessman, not an untrustworthy playboy condemned by his father as not worthy to hold so much as a share in the Kingsleigh empire. So he'd take no risks now; he did not want stories about his personal life circulating.

So he kept his voice casual. 'Would you mind dropping Lily and I to Jemaa el-Fnaa? The night is young and it seems like a good idea to visit.'

He hoped the suggestion sounded natural— after all Jemaa el-Fnaa was a tourist must-see, a historic square with atmospheric appeal full of street entertainers, food and market stalls. It was meant to come alive at night.

'Of course,' Natalia said and to his relief Lily made no demur. 'If you are there, seeing as you missed dessert, go and have pancakes. Aline is part of our family and it is her first night trading there. I'll draw you a map so you can find her.'

'That sounds great. Thank you, Natalia.'

Fifteen minutes later Natalia pulled to a stop and he and Lily climbed out of the car. Lily waited until the car had receded into the distance then frowned. 'Why did you suggest this?'

'I can't be sure, but I think we were followed here from the restaurant. I reckoned, if I'm right, this is the perfect place to lose them.'

Lily glanced around. 'Do you really think someone would bother following us?'

'Possibly. Unfortunately, the press does have a massive interest in my private life and, whilst it's not a big deal, I'm sure you don't want to feature as my "mystery date", so why take the risk? Plus, this square is a must-see part of the city.'

Lily nodded. 'I have read about it and it sounds like a real experience. There are so many things to do here. I think I'll have to come back on holiday one day and go on a hot-air-balloon ride and visit the desert, but right now this sounds good.'

They stepped forward, and he was as careful as she to keep a distance between them as they approached the entrance. He heard her give a small gasp and instinctively step closer to him.

'Wow,' she said. And he knew what she meant. The square was a cacophony of noise, an overwhelming mix of people and smells that hit the senses all at once. Stalls selling food were dotted everywhere, smoke, steam and tantalising smells all rising and mingling in the air.

There were the shouts of the vendors, calling attention to their wares, English and Arabic interspersing. The number of people was mindboggling, making the whole a mass and mixture of humanity, tourists intermingled with locals. Music, drums, rock guitars and singing all blended the air with motes of noise and he closed his eyes to separate and distinguish the notes.

When he opened them, he saw Lily alight with enthusiasm, the planes and angles of her face lit by the flares of light that illuminated the darkness 'It's...amazing. I don't know where to look first or where to start or...anything.' She looked round. 'If we get separated, let's meet back here. Provided we can find it.'

In the meantime, he realised all they could do was stay close, and he steeled himself to do that without showing any reaction. He reminded himself that they were simply part of a crowd of people who were all in close proximity. But as they walked nothing, even the buzz of activity—the sight of snake charmers, people with trained monkeys, the vibrant colours and eye-catching goods on display—could completely dim his awareness of the woman by his side, the lively interest on her face, the gloss of her hair as it bobbed on the curve of her shoulder, her graceful light-footed tread or the sway of her body...

They came to a natural stop at a tent where a man stood, probably in his sixties, dressed in a long, dark-red robe, a knitted hat on his head. As they paused he stepped forward and greeted the gathering crowds.

'He's a story-teller,' a woman next to Darius said. 'He's telling the story of the Arabian nights.' A minute later, the man started to speak, his voice rich and compelling, seeming to weave the story in the air.

Darius glanced down at Lily and saw she was as transfixed as he. Somehow it didn't matter that they couldn't understand the actual words; the beauty of the language, the narrator's sweeping gestures and detailed actions all contributed to the telling of the story, painting a picture of magical hues and nuances, depth and meaning.

The story-teller was a man who had clearly done this job for decades, his grizzled hair and weather-beaten face a testament to his years and experience. His voice was low, deep and mesmerising as he spoke and the beauty of the words washed over them.

Darius was reminded of his mother's voice when she had told him stories, those few precious good moments in a childhood of uncertainty and survival. Times when she had perhaps only had a few hits of alcohol or drugs, or the best times of all, the times of hope, when she tried to stop. She'd sat with him on the tattered, stained sofa and woven him magical stories, her imagination coming up with characters he could remember to this day—daring, swashbuckling heroes and heroines who lived in worlds populated by pirates, wizards and magic. He wondered where she was now, and wished that he could turn around and see her telling a story in one of the stalls—beautiful, wistful, magical. But that wasn't going to happen.

The man came to an end and there were protests from the audience. The man next to them shook his head and turned to them. 'It's a good way of doing it. He's stopped on a cliff-hanger so we're all bound to come back tomorrow.'

'That was amazing,' Lily said.

Looking down at her, Darius wondered what she was thinking and whether this had transported her back to *her* childhood. 'Like a fairy tale.'

'No. Or at least, not like the fairy tales I used to believe in.'

He heard the slight note of bitterness in her voice. 'So you don't believe any more?'

'I'm a believer in stories where real people control their own fate and don't rely on happiness being provided by a handsome prince based on some mistaken idea of love. I mean, really? Cinderella meets the man of her dreams all because a fairy godmother waves a magic wand to transform her into someone beautiful? Do you think the handsome prince would even have noticed Cinderella if he'd walked past her in her rags, holding a mop? He wouldn't have given her a second glance, or if he had it would have been to order her to clean the floor. But once he thought she was a lady, all dressed up in a fancy gown with her hair done…when she looked beautiful…then it's different.

'On top of that they have a dance together and that's it, he falls in love? Hah! He only fell for her because she ran away from him, all because she thought he wouldn't like her if she wasn't in a proper dress. I mean, why would you fall for a man who only likes you if you're in a ball gown? And did you notice fairy tales all end with "they all lived happily ever after"? No detail… More likely the handsome prince had his head turned by another beautiful lady at the very next ball.'

She came to a halt and he studied her flushed face, sensing that her words had come straight from her heart.

'I can see you've given this some thought,' he said.

'Actually, I have. You can laugh but, whilst I think stories are incredibly important, fairy tales spin an unrealistic picture. "Happy ever after" does not need to involve love. Everyone deserves happiness, not just those who fate and genes have given good looks to.'

'I'm not laughing,' he said gently. 'I promise.' After all, he didn't believe in fairy tales either. Think of his own story: abandoned by his mother, he'd been rescued by his father, a wealthy, handsome prince indeed; a king of an empire. That should have panned out into a happy ever after, but it had been a whole lot more complicated than that. 'I don't believe in fairy tales either. I believe in making your own happy ending on your terms.'

Now she looked up at him, perhaps caught by the unintended seriousness of his words, the hard intent he hadn't managed to hide.

There was a small frown on her face, her dark-blue eyes full of questions, her mobile face framed by the glossy hair, and there it was again: that *whoomph* of attraction; that desire to kiss her; that flare of desire that she could ignite so easily and instantaneously.

He forced himself to move and forced his lips to upturn into a light smile. 'Now, what would make me happy is a pancake,' he said. 'Shall we try and find Aline's stall?'

Lily nodded and they slipped back into the throng of people strolling through the square. But now, instead of looking at all the stalls and sights, he found his eyes dragged inexorably back to Lily. He realised that she was glancing at him, and every intercepted look, every awkward turn away, heightened the simmer of awareness, the tug and pull of a connection he didn't want or understand but couldn't seem to break.

'I think this must be it,' he said, aware his voice had an edge to it as he gestured to a stall that already had a long queue.

'It looks busy,' she said. 'That's great for Aline on her first day.'

Darius opened his mouth to answer then heard a shout from the front of the queue. Before he could see what was happening, he heard

Lily give an exclamation, and then she was off, moving towards the source of the noise.

Darius followed, hampered by the craning necks of others trying to work out what was going on. He firmly pushed his way through and came to a stop as he quickly digested the scene: two men, tourists who had clearly had a few glasses too many, were right at the edge of the stall, one of them shouting at the stall owner, a slight woman who was trying to placate them. He could see real fear in her eyes, and sensed on some level that this woman had been hurt before... A sudden memory flashed into his brain of himself as a boy, cowering before one of his mum's boyfriends.

Then from nowhere Lily emerged, clearly utterly unafraid as she strode up to the man, and Darius felt a tug of admiration.

'Is there a problem?' Her voice was crystal-clear.

'Yes, lady, there is a problem and I'm dealing with it. I've been waiting fifteen minutes. I'm fed up and I'm talking to this incompetent here, asking her what she's gonna do about it. So get out of my way.'

Lily stood her ground, seemingly not even aware as Darius stepped forward. 'I don't think so. I heard what you said to her and it was unacceptable.' Her voice was tight with outrage, etched with disdain.

'I'm warning you to mind your own business or...'

'Or what?' Darius kept his voice calm and his eye on the crowd. He saw the man's companion step forward in an aggressive lurch and heard the murmur as others too seemed ready to enter the fray. He knew security patrolled the square but he had no idea how long they would take to get here.

'Or I'll move her out of the way myself.'

Lily stepped forward. 'I don't think so,' she said, seemingly still unfazed by the man's threatening tone.

'Neither do I.' Darius raised his voice. 'But I think we all have a choice here. I don't want a fight, but I won't let you hurt anyone.' His voice was hard; he might not have been able to protect himself or his mother aged seven, but he damn well could defend himself now. 'But I'd also rather not be dragged off by security to the local police station. So how about you get back into the queue and wait for your pancake?'

There was a pause and he could see the man thinking. 'Argh! Stuff the pancakes,' he said. 'We're taking our business elsewhere. With that he left, and Darius saw Lily suddenly falter, as if the adrenalin that had been fuelling her had suddenly run dry.

'Are you OK?' he asked, moving towards her.

'Yes... I... It...' She took a deep breath. 'I'm fine. More to the point, we need to see if Aline is all right. She headed towards the stall owner and Darius followed.

'Thank you for the help,' Aline said, a faint tremble in her voice.

'No problem. We've just come from Jamal and Natalia,' Darius said. 'Natalia told us to try a pancake.'

'I am glad you were here. Please, if you will wait, I will make you both a pancake, but first...'

'First,' Lily said, 'You have a lot of customers. I think you could use some help. I'll stay until the queue gets more manageable.'

Darius blinked; a lot of women he knew would have felt they had done enough and would have suggested that Aline pack up and finish early. Instead, Lily was offering practical help. Perhaps because she knew what it was like to start out and set up a business, and so did he. Knew too the sense of despair when it felt as though an idea wasn't going to work.

'Good idea,' Darius said. 'How shall we do

it? I'm happy to take orders and manage the money. Or I can help out with the pancakes?'

Surprise touched Lily's face and Darius knew she'd assumed he'd walk away. She probably thought he'd consider helping on a stall to be beneath him or something. Frustration touched him at the judgment, though perhaps he should be pleased. Her assumptions about who he was were at least a barrier to help keep attraction at bay. Yet it rankled.

Then she smiled, a smile that held a sudden warmth that seemed to flood him with a sense of happiness. 'It makes more sense if I help with the cooking,' she said.

'Sure. We can swap after a while.'

'But…' Aline looked a bit taken aback. 'You don't have to. I can manage.'

'We want to,' Darius said briskly.

Aline hesitated, looked at the queue and then nodded. 'Thank you.'

Soon enough they got into a rhythm. Darius got his head round the unfamiliar currency, and he could see that Lily and Aline had worked out the best way to work in tandem. He watched as Aline visibly relaxed, smiled even; he also saw how hard Lily worked. Never once did she look resentful, or as though she wished she were somewhere else. Respect and admiration touched him at her genuine kindness as two hours sped past, the queue started to die down and around them stall holders started to shut up shop.

'I don't know how to thank you,' Aline said softly. 'Please let me pay you or…'

'Absolutely not,' Lily said firmly. 'Your family gave us an amazing meal on the house. This can be our payback.'

Aline hesitated. 'Please do not tell Jamal about what happened. I had a helper lined up but he couldn't make it today. He will be here tomorrow, so this won't happen again, so there is no need for Jamal to worry. He is not really my family and he has already helped me and others like me so much. He runs a scheme for young adults who have had…difficulties in life.'

The young woman's voice was deliberately devoid of all emotion, the words said carefully, as if she had rehearsed them many times to try to make them more palatable. 'He takes us in and teaches us how to cook. I…owe him a lot and now I want him to see that I have succeeded, not that I am weak and need more help.'

'Needing help doesn't make you weak,' Lily said softly.

'It doesn't,' Darius said. 'But I understand

you want to show Jamal that you can stand on your own two feet. So how about we make a deal? We agree not to tell Jamal, but if your helper can't make it tomorrow you either tell us and we will help out or you call Jamal and ask him.'

'Promise us that you won't do this alone tomorrow,' Lily said.

'I promise.' Aline's voice was fervent. 'Thank you for understanding. Now, really you can go.' She waved. 'I have someone coming to pick me up and take me home—here he is now. '

They waited until the man approached and greeted Aline, then they said their goodbyes and headed towards the exit.

'That was nice of you,' Lily said after a silence that had felt companionable, two people walking after a job well done.

'What was?'

'All of it—getting involved.' She puffed out a sigh. 'We were meant to be getting lost in the crowd, keeping a low profile. I'm sorry.'

'You've nothing to apologise for. You didn't ask that man to get aggressive and you didn't ask me to step in. You were doing pretty well by yourself. It was brave of you to confront him and defend Aline.' It really had been; her desire to protect a woman she didn't know had impressed itself on him, all the more because she didn't seem to rate it as unusual or praiseworthy herself.

'It wasn't brave, not really. I did it on instinct. Aline looked terrified, and that man was a bully, nothing more. Bullies prey on those they perceive to be vulnerable—the key is not to show fear even if you are feeling it. It doesn't necessarily stop them, but they feed off fear.'

She pressed her lips together, as if she'd said too much, and he wondered if she was speaking from her own experience. If Aline's experience had resonated with her in the same way it had done with him on a personal level. 'Thank you for stepping up, for supporting me.'

'Did you think I'd run away?' That truly rankled.

'No. I thought you'd go and get security rather than risk being recognised. And I definitely didn't expect you to help serve pancakes all night.' She paused. 'Why did you?'

'Why did I help? Because I wanted to help her.' It was that simple. He'd sensed a kinship with Aline, even before she'd hinted at a childhood of difficulty. He knew what that felt like. 'And I admire what she is doing. A difficult childhood sometimes leads to a lifetime of difficulty, getting into trouble. She is making something of her life, and I get that she wants to do it on her own—prove herself.'

'That she can stand on her own two feet.'

'Yes.' They looked at each other and, almost against his will, Darius smiled and Lily smiled back. He had a sudden urge to pull her into his arms, but of course he didn't. Instead, he glanced at his watch. 'We'd better get back. Where are you staying? We'll get a taxi and I'll drop you off first.'

There was a silence and Lily's eyes widened. 'Actually, I don't know. Gemma was going to sort that out and with…everything this evening I totally forgot. But it's fine. I'll stay in the villa.'

'No.' Darius had no intention of letting her do anything of the sort. 'It's nearly midnight and the lock isn't even reliable. I'll book you into my hotel.' He frowned. 'In fact, I took over Gemma's booking, so she may well have booked you a room there anyway.'

He pulled out his phone and called the hotel. 'Darius Kingsleigh here. Can I check whether Gemma Fairley-Godfrey made a booking for my colleague, Lily Culpepper?' A minute later he put his phone back in his pocket and nodded. 'All sorted. You're already on the system. Where's your luggage?'

'At the villa. But I can manage until tomorrow, assuming I can get a toothbrush from somewhere.'

'I'm sure the hotel supplies all that.'

'Then let's go.'

CHAPTER SIX

TEN MINUTES LATER they walked down a cobbled alley and into a courtyard that housed a majestic, sprawling rose-pink building more akin to a stately home than a hotel. They followed the illuminated mosaic pathway to the entrance. The lobby was an expanse of splendour with marble floors and imposing pillars tiled in tiny mosaic tiles, surrounded by intricate plaster work. The walls were covered in an opulence of mirrors and panels.

As they stood at the vast reception desk Lily tried to think, her head awhirl with the day's events as she looked at Darius. Impossible now to hold on to the original antipathy she'd felt for him, however hard she tried. Because, however dubious his morals might be in his relationships, he had exhibited nothing but courtesy and kindness to Jamal, Natalia and Aline.

He'd stood by her side and seen off the bullies, and his presence had steadied her, helped her stand her ground. She'd been aware of a warmth at seeing his protective instinct, and seeing his willingness to help Aline had helped her repel her own memories triggered by seeing Aline's fear. It had been a reminder of how fearful she had once been at the mercy of her stepsisters. But she didn't want to see Darius as a knight in shining armour, and didn't want to like him; that would make the unwanted attraction even more complicated.

A man approached them, a smile on his face. 'Mr Kingsleigh, it is good to see you. And you must be Ms Culpepper. I will show you both to your suite.'

Suite? Singular?

Darius frowned. 'I assumed Ms Culpepper had a separate room booked.'

'No. Lady Fairley-Godfrey booked a suite as that was all we had available. But there are two bedrooms and two bathrooms. We have no other free rooms. Will this be all right?'

Darius looked across at Lily and she tried to keep her face composed. Two *en suite* rooms in one suite: it was no different from having two separate rooms, not really. Yet the idea felt too…intimate, too close, too much. But she could hardly say that; after all, if it were any other professional colleague she wouldn't have had an issue with this.

'That sounds fine,' she said.

'Then I will show you the way.' They followed him along rug-covered floors surrounded by crimson walls and wrought-iron lanterns that illuminated the detailed woodwork, the glass cabinets that encased vases, bowls and sculptures, until they arrived at their suite.

The door was opened with a flourish. Lily stopped on the threshold and blinked at the sheer splendour of the room. Massive chandeliers hung from vaulted ceilings, and brass lanterns illuminated and shadowed the aubergine-coloured walls adorned with art deco mirrors with silver-and-gilt swirls. The furniture was resplendent regency style, padded with purple velvet, whilst heavy-swagged crimson curtains framed stained-glass windows and doors leading onto a private balcony.

The staff member walked forward and pulled open the bedroom doors to reveal similarly styled bedrooms, both containing king-size beds and walk-in wardrobes, the floors covered with Moroccan rugs and the walls stencilled with safari animals. Further inspection revealed enormous bathrooms with golden sinks, whirlpool baths and sumptuously soft towels.

'Thank you,' Lily managed. 'This all looks wonderful.'

The manager smiled and soon after he departed, leaving Lily and Darius to regard each other in silence.

Darius studied her face. 'Are you truly all right with this?'

'Yes.' She strove to put sincerity into the syllable. She refused to acknowledge that she felt edgy, not because she didn't trust him, but perhaps because she didn't trust herself. The unwanted attraction, the sense that something had shifted over the evening and a sense of intimacy were all messing with her head. But she wouldn't let it. She was a professional; Darius was a business colleague. 'Completely. I'm looking forward to getting to work.'

His grey eyes remained on her face. 'How about we start now? We could sit on the balcony and have a cup of tea.'

Lily gave a sudden smile; she couldn't help it.

'What?'

'Nothing. I just didn't associate the idea of "a cup of tea" with Darius Kingsleigh.'

'Nothing wrong with a good old-fashioned

cuppa,' he said. 'Proper tea that a spoon can stand up in, that's what my mum used to say.' He caught his lip between his teeth and she sensed he hadn't meant to say that, though he continued smoothly enough. 'But, in this case, it is mint tea on offer, if that's OK?'

'That's fine, and I'd love to start planning now,' she said, suddenly aware of how little she knew about him. She knew he'd been taken in by his natural father Enzo Kingsleigh as a child. That had stuck in her head simply because it had been a childhood fantasy of her own: that her natural father would somehow discover her existence and track her down, even though she knew the impossibility of that happening. But she knew nothing about his mother; she couldn't recall any mention of Darius's life before Enzo.

She watched as Darius made the tea, looking at the deft movements, the curve of his forearm and the lithe breadth of his body. Her tummy clenched with sudden intense desire and she looked away and went out to wait on the balcony. Looked out at the view of the illuminated courtyard, complete with mosaic floors, and a water fountain providing a musical flow of water against a backdrop of potted plants and marbled pillars. The whole place was deserted and she assumed it was either closed overnight or was only for private use.

Darius brought out a tray and placed it on the table, before sitting opposite her. She concentrated on pouring the tea, hoping her hands wouldn't tremble.

'Right,' she said. 'We need to work out what order to do things in and how best to divide and share different tasks. Obviously, we need to clean the villa. I didn't have much of a chance to look over it earlier, but I could see it is quite a mammoth task. I may need to get extra help.'

'That's no problem. We can hire professional cleaners.'

'I also want to go the local souks to get local soaps and shampoos that we can try out, and then pick and choose for the guests. And I need to inventory plates, glasses and so on.'

'We also need caterers.'

Lily sipped the tea as ideas started to fizz and pop in her head. 'For the canapés, we could ask real street vendors to put up their stalls at the villa itself, perhaps in the courtyard, and we could get waiting staff to carry the food to the guests.'

'I like it.' His face lit now with an enthusiasm that mirrored her own. 'Aline could do pancakes, and maybe some of Jamal's other protégé chefs could run stalls.'

'Jamal and his team could cater the sit-down dinner.'

'We can make it a really authentic Marrakesh-themed event.'

'Yes, set a stage up, have a storyteller—maybe a local dance troupe—then clear the floor and have a band and dancing.'

Adrenalin surged through her. 'It's a plan.'

'It's better than that. It's an awesome plan.' He rose to his feet. 'And it deserves something more than tea.'

Once he'd exited the balcony, Lily rose to her feet, energised by the brainstorming session and the way they'd sparked off each other. Glancing at her watch, she saw how late it was and yet she wasn't tired. She leant against the railings, turning as he re-joined her and handed her a glass of champagne. She gestured to the view—the traditional architecture, the magical flow of the waterfall, the intricate design of the tiles— and inhaled the scent of orange blossom that pervaded the air. 'Midnight in Marrakesh,' she said. 'Isn't it beautiful?'

'Yes,' he said, his voice deep, and heat touched her face as she realised he wasn't looking at the courtyard. He was looking at her. He raised his champagne glass. 'To us.'

'To us,' she echoed. They both sipped, and now it wasn't only her brain that hummed. Moonlight glinted, highlighting his dark hair with a coppery sheen, and she could see the swell of muscle, the craggy features and his eyes, silvery-grey now as they met hers.

Something shifted, the silver-grey darkened, his eyes full of intent and promise. She could see desire and sense the swirl, pull and lure of attraction, a magnet inexorably pulling her in. Her feet moved forward without her permission, and then he also stepped forward, and somehow the glass was no longer in her hand; it was on the table and she was in his arms.

Anticipation and butterflies skittered around her tummy in a flotilla, and a shiver flitted over her skin. Then he lowered his mouth onto hers; the feel of his lips against hers unleashed a need, a yearning for more that it was impossible to deny. Not when he was so close with the scent of him, the taste of him, the feel of his body against hers.

Her lips parted and then he kissed her for real and she was lost, lost in the swirling tornado of desire and heat. She pressed against the hard, muscular length of his body and now her arms were looped round his neck.

The distant blare of a horn broke the spell and Lily pulled away, jumped back and stood still, breath ragged in the night air. What had she done? What about professionalism? Hell, she'd practically plastered herself all over him.

She had no idea what to do, what to say or how to retrieve the situation. 'Sorry,' she blurted and, turning, she half-walked, half-ran towards the suite. The best thing, the only thing, to do right now was hide. Work out a plan, a way to erase the past ten minutes: find some dignity.

Darius watched her go, and tried to work out what to do next, but his brain seemed incapable of rational thought. His whole being was still caught up in the kiss, a kiss that had blown his mind; every sense was heightened, his body still on high alert, taut with frustrated desire. A desire he had to dampen, ignore, get rid of.

He hadn't meant to kiss her, but it had been impossible not to. She'd been so beautiful, so infinitely desirable, her eyes sparkling in the moonlight, her passion for the job spilling over; she had been irresistible.

He'd broken all the rules. They were working together, and he'd known she felt uncomfortable staying in the same suite. He wouldn't blame Lily for leaving and quitting the job.

Guilt touched him. Why did this attraction have such power? Perhaps it was a simple case of timing—he hadn't been on so much as a date in the past two years. But it felt more than that—something visceral with a mind of its own—and that made him edgy. He couldn't turn back the clock, couldn't erase that kiss. But he could ensure that it wouldn't happen again. How hard could it be *not* to kiss someone?

Should he go and try and talk to her? He couldn't—to go and knock on her bedroom door would send the wrong signal completely. The only thing to do was to wait until morning. Then he'd apologise, assure her that he would not overstep the professional boundary again. And he wouldn't.

All he could do now was try to sleep…a state he eventually achieved, only to be woken by a banging on his door what seemed like minutes later.

He opened his eyes, instantly awake, and swung his legs out of the bed, tugged on his jeans, grabbed a T-shirt, made his way to the door and pulled it open.

'Are you OK? What's wrong?'

'I…' She stepped back and heat touched her cheeks as her gaze focused on his bare chest; he'd swear she gulped. 'Everything is wrong.'

'Can you be more specific?' He tugged the T-shirt over his head. 'Tell me.' Lily's blue eyes were full of panic. 'Define "everything"…'

CHAPTER SEVEN

LILY DIDN'T KNOW where to begin, but she did know everything really had gone horribly wrong.

She wasn't sure how long her phone had rung for, but she'd grabbed it, half-asleep, her head filled with fuzzy dreams featuring Darius and that kiss. She'd opened her eyes to take in the grandeur of her surroundings.

'Mum?' She'd wondered why Maria would be calling her at this hour. 'Is everything OK?'

'Well, darling, you tell me. I'm calling to congratulate you. You've finally taken my advice and made a fabulous conquest.'

'Huh?' The first tendril of panic had started to unfold.

'Darius Kingsleigh.'

'I told you I had dinner with a client. That client is Darius Kingsleigh.'

Maria had laughed, a deep and dirty chuckle. 'Well, sweetheart, if that's a client you're in a different profession than I thought. I think you should have a look at the pictures on social media.'

So Lily had done exactly that, and then she'd panicked big-time, leapt out of bed and now here they were.

'So?' Darius asked. 'What's going on?' There was a knot of impatience in his voice now and Lily gestured to the round glass table in the middle of the room, then went and sat down.

'We've been spotted. There are pictures of us from this evening…including the kiss.'

Darius did some inventive swearing, pulled out his phone, scrolled down, closed his eyes and opened them again. 'OK. This isn't good.'

'You think?' Lily shook her head. 'It's… disastrous.' Her tummy churned with horror at the situation. Everything had been bad enough before but at least then the only person she'd been hiding from was Darius. Now she wanted to hide from the whole world but there was nowhere to hide.

He drummed his fingers on the table and she took some comfort from the fact he seemed to grasp the scale of the disaster. 'Then we have to turn disaster into something palatable.'

'Palatable?' she echoed. 'There is nothing palatable about this.' She gestured to his phone, holder of the proof, pictures that even now people were looking at. 'Denial isn't going to work, is it?'

'No.'

'Then what are we going to do?' She rose to her feet and started to pace, her mind spinning. 'What am *I* going to do?' Ramifications and scenarios all whirled through her head. 'My family, my friends, my *clients* are going to see those pictures…of me plastered all over *you*. That is mortifying. They are going to think…'

That she was shallow, that she was a gold-digger, that she wanted her five seconds of fame, happy to be another proverbial notch on his bed post, another in a line of women…

Worse. 'Oh, God, you are my client. People are going to think I sleep with my clients! They may even think that I got this job because of that. My professional reputation will go down the pan.' Her stride increased with each word, hands clenched, jaw set, and then she came up against Darius. She came to a halt, looked up at him and tried to read his expression.

'Lily, slow down.'

'I can't slow down. And I can't think of a solution.' Lily inhaled deeply. It was time to pull herself together; she'd spent her life working out coping strategies. She'd coped with not knowing who her dad was, with her mother's lifestyle, with the bullying of her stepsisters and the heartbreak and humiliation of her break-up with Tom. Now it was time to stop acting like a drama queen and work out how to cope with this.

'Sorry,' she said. 'I just hate the idea that that kiss is out there being pored over, and I hate how it's going to impact my business.'

'I get that,' he said. 'Truly I do.' Lily studied his expression and heard the sincerity. 'We'll work this out,' he continued. 'But not here. If the press really decide to jump on it, they'll start making a nuisance of themselves here.'

He drummed his fingers on his thigh and she found her gaze fixated on the movement, on the strength of his fingers, the muscular sturdiness of the denim-clad muscle. 'I suggest we move.' He glanced at his watch. 'We can sneak out the back, mingle with the crowds and come up with a strategy.'

'That didn't work so well yesterday,' she pointed out.

'No, but yesterday someone at the restaurant must have tipped the photographer off...said where we were going. Yesterday I wasn't really even sure we were being followed. Today is different, and today they know we are here.'

'Then let's get out of here.'

* * *

Fifteen minutes later Darius glanced round quickly as they left the hotel into a deserted alleyway.

'You've obviously done this before,' Lily said, pulling the brim of her sun hat down slightly.

'The important thing to do is look as though you belong, that you're just another tourist out for a look at early-morning Marrakesh.'

'OK. I'll try.'

'I know how worried you are about this.' He knew and understood her concerns. It didn't look good to be caught on camera in a thoroughly unprofessional, passionate clinch with your client, not for her and not for him. Anger at himself propelled his stride; those pictures hardly portrayed the businessman's persona he had worked so hard to show the world. Instead, they'd reignite his playboy image, and it couldn't be worse timing.

He glanced at his watch. 'Let's head to one of the city gardens,' he said. 'Find somewhere secluded to talk.'

Tickets purchased, they headed across the turquoise-blue mosaic courtyard past an array of plants. Rosemary from the hedges scented the air, along with a citrus aroma. Different hues of green contrasted and blended into a verdant oasis, succulents, grass and trees all combining to create an aura of tranquillity and peace.

'This is a good place to think,' she said as they sat on a secluded bench. 'Or at least I hope it is. Otherwise maybe I could stay right here until this all goes away.'

He could see the worry in her dark-blue eyes and guilt touched him. Damn it—he'd known there was a risk of publicity but last night he hadn't given it a thought. Kissing Lily had seemed so right, so inevitable, and desire had taken over thought or reason.

And so he'd handed over a story all because he hadn't been able to control this damned attraction. Now they were both up the proverbial creek and he'd better find a paddle. He closed his eyes, welcoming the heat of the early-morning sunshine on his face, and allowed his mind to roam, to think. Desperation galvanised his thought process, planting the seeds of a plan. 'I've got an idea,' he said.

'Go ahead,'

'We fake a relationship. We already set the scene in the restaurant last night. Jamal and his family already believe we are a genuine couple. We say that you were hired for the role by Gemma, Gemma introduced us, *then* we became a couple, so Gemma suggested we come to Morocco together. That way you would have been hired before you even met me, when Gemma was the client.'

There was a silence and then she sighed, shaking her head. 'It's a good idea, but it wouldn't work.'

'Why not?'

'You. And me?' Another shake. 'It couldn't happen.'

'Why not?'

'Because it simply doesn't work. I wouldn't date you and you wouldn't date me.'

'I hate to be repetitive but…why not?'

'For a start, you date beautiful celebrities. I'm neither.'

There it was again, that faint but unmistakable hint of disapproval and, damn it, it still irked him, put him on the back foot. 'You're right that I've only ever dated celebrities, but there are reasons for that. When you're a millionaire, it makes sense to date women who you know aren't after your money, or only with you for the lifestyle. People who have money and status of their own. People who are used to being in the public eye and enjoy it, who aren't phased by the attention. So, yes, I deliberately chose to date people like that, but that doesn't mean I wouldn't date a non-celebrity.'

'And I'm not beautiful.' Her gaze met his full-on. 'I'm not fishing for compliments, it's a fact. Like most people, I'm not super-model material. And I don't have any "it factor".'

Darius stared at her. 'To me, you are beautiful.' Seeing the scepticism on her face, he continued, wanting her to know that was truth. 'That's what attraction is: it's nothing to do with "super-model" beauty. Sure, a few people have universal appeal because of their looks or status. They will turn heads when they enter a room, but that's neither here nor there. That's not individual "it factor", the real thing.' He looked at her, saw she was looking down at the table, knew that for some reason Lily didn't believe him. 'Look at me,' he said softly. 'That kiss last night, that was the real thing.'

And in that moment he relived it again, and so did she. He could see it in her slightly parted lips and in the widened dark-blue eyes that skimmed over his own lips and lingered before she looked back at him. She raised a hand to her lips, as if she could feel remembered sensations.

'The real thing can happen between any two people, beautiful or not, famous or not…a genuine chemistry that is unique to them. It's not explicable, but it's there, and it can be ignited by a brush of the hands, a laugh, a look, a smile…' He shrugged. 'We have that, and that is obvious. People will believe we are a couple—a proper couple.' Now his brain was firing. 'In fact, it's *better* that you aren't a celebrity.'

She eyed him with more than a hint of scepticism. 'Why?'

'Because if we portray ourselves as being in an actual real relationship, not a fling or a one-night stand but something *serious*, that takes away the stigma of being unprofessional.' It would allow him to use the publicity to counter his playboy image and show he'd evolved. 'I think we can pull this off. What do you think?'

It was a good question that Lily didn't know the answer to; her brain still fogged with the volatile swirl of emotions, a sense of the surreal, enhanced by his statement that their chemistry was real, that the kiss had been the real thing. Lily couldn't help it; that knowledge sent a thrill through her veins that the burn of need and yearning had been mutual.

What was wrong with her? This wasn't about desire; this was about salvaging her business reputation that was at stake because she'd given in to an unprofessional attraction. So, would Darius's idea work?

She closed her eyes and tried to imagine pretending to be in a relationship with Darius—the speculation, the publicity, being seen as a woman either foolish enough to fall for a playboy's charms, or a gold-digger chasing wealth and fame. The idea was abhorrent.

But the alternative was worse—being seen as a woman who slept with her clients in order to win business, or simply casually slept with them willy-nilly, with no thought of professional ethics and boundaries.

She was caught between a rock and a hard place, but in truth the choice was obvious. She would not let her business suffer, because nothing meant more to her than the business she had built up. It was solid, incontrovertible proof that she had succeeded when no one, including her, had believed she would. The bullying at school had knocked her confidence to sub-zero levels and it had had a disastrous impact on her studies. The number of times her school work had been ruined… The lack of sleep because she was too terrified to close her eyes, an inability to concentrate in class, had all resulted in grades that portrayed her as an unqualified failure.

Left behind at home whilst, thankfully, her stepsisters had gone on to further education, she'd found a job as a cleaner.

Her mother had thrown up her hands in despair yet again. 'But why, darling? Let me send you to a different type of school, with Cynthia—one where they teach you how to make the best of yourself. Then you can win yourself a man, and kaboom!'

Those words had crystallised in Lily a determination to succeed in her own right; she'd worked all hours, saved and eventually launched her own company. She'd built a reputation and a client base that now included Lady Gemma Fairley-Godfrey. No way would she jeopardise any of that—not over some hormonal reaction. If she had to fake a relationship, then so be it. She'd messed up: she'd pay the price.

'I'll do it,' she said, hearing the reluctance in her voice.

He studied her face. 'I said we *could* pull it off. We won't be able to if you feel so much antipathy to the idea.'

Lily sighed. 'You can hardly expect me to be enthusiastic,' she pointed out. 'Our attraction may exist but it's landed us in a complete mess. And I am now going to have to fake feelings for you when…'

'You don't even like me?' he suggested, and she'd swear there was a hint of hurt in his voice.

'When I don't even know you,' she said. 'But it's not that. People will class me as a fool for falling for a playboy or believe I am a gold-digger. Then, when we end it, I will be seen as another discarded girlfriend.'

'I don't discard my girlfriends. I don't discard anyone. My relationships are short-term but that's through mutual agreement.' His voice was even, but she could hear anger in it, but knew that she couldn't let him get away with that statement.

'What about Ruby AllStar?' Lily recalled reading about the break-up, the article etched in her memory. She'd been sitting in her bed under the duvet, a tub of chocolate-chip ice-cream by her side, desperately trying not to relive the bitter humiliation of her own break-up with Tom. Trying not to let the scene replay again and again, trying not to let his words repeat on loop…

'I'm sorry, Lily, truly. I never meant this to happen.'

Her own words: 'Can't you see? Cynthia is using you… She's taken you to hurt me.'

His reply: 'Maybe. But, if I'd truly loved you, I wouldn't have been available to be taken. Whatever happens with Cynthia and I… I can't have loved you.'

His voice had been gentle and she'd seen sadness and finality in his brown eyes. And, worst of all, she'd seen pity.

When she'd read the interview with Ruby AllStar, outlining her feelings after being 'discarded' by Darius Kingsleigh, Lily had identified with the singer's obvious heartbreak, the details resonating with her own situation.

'You broke her heart,' she said now and, seeing his lips set in a tight line, knew she'd touched a nerve. 'Led her on to believe you meant commitment. Strung her along, made promises you had no intention of keeping.'

'And you know this how—from one interview?'

Lily opened her mouth and closed it again.

'You are basing your entire opinion on one woman's version of events, letting her rewrite history.'

His words collided with her anger as their truth hit her. Letting one woman rewrite history: as her stepsisters had written theirs, making the bullying, fear and terror they'd inspired into something trivial, almost jokey. Making everyone accept their version of events so no one was inclined to listen to Lily's side, let alone believe it. Until even Lily had started to question events and her own memories.

Had that happened to Darius? As far as she knew, he'd never refuted Ruby's claims, and had never given his side, even as speculation, accusations and opinion pieces had run rife. But that didn't mean it didn't exist.

'You're right,' she said now. 'Tell me your version.'

Darius hadn't expected that, had thought Lily would double down. He'd never told anyone the truth about Ruby, but he wanted to tell Lily. To his own annoyance her accusation had set him on edge, and he suspected that this was the crux of her disapproval of him, her judgment. If they were going to fake a relationship, they had to get past it. But, more than that, he *wanted* to overturn her judgment, remove the hint of disapproval in her dealings with him.

He took a moment and then began. 'My relationship with Ruby started like all my others. I explained up front that all I was looking for was a short-term, fun relationship that had no chance of leading to anything serious. And Ruby agreed to that. I wouldn't have gone on a second date if she hadn't or if I didn't believe her.'

'Then what happened?'

He hesitated. 'From my point of view, nothing. I thought everything was on track, that we were having fun. We got to the ten-week mark and I was about to suggest we bring things to the agreed end. Ruby was on tour so I waited until she got back. I assumed she'd been expecting it. Instead, she got really upset. Said she thought that, because we'd exceeded ten weeks, she thought she was different, that I loved her and wanted something long-term. She told me she'd changed, wanted more…that she loved me.'

He could remember the sense of horror along with sheer bewilderment, his weak attempts to justify, explain, when she'd asked how he could abandon her. An echo of the question he'd asked himself about his mother all his life.

'Didn't you realise, see any signs?' There was scepticism in Lily's tone and he couldn't really blame her.

'No, I truly didn't. If I had, I would have done something, ended it sooner at the very least. I had no intention of hurting Ruby.'

He'd never wanted to hurt any woman and he'd decided the best way to do that was never to commit. Because he knew he didn't get it, didn't have what it took. How could he? He'd believed his mum loved him and she'd left; he'd spent years, decades, trying to win his father's love and had failed. Darius was bright enough to know a background like that did not give anyone a good start in the love stakes, knew he wasn't capable of long-term commitment. 'I know I got it wrong. I miscalculated.'

'This isn't about calculations, it's about feelings.'

'I don't understand feelings. I understand calculations, programming. Feelings are too messy, too complicated, too risky. I don't want any of that. Which is why I don't look for long-term relationships and why I *agree* terms up front. The other person needs to be on board too. Ruby was at the start and then she changed the rules, rewrote the terms and made it into a story, an illusion.'

'She didn't change the terms. Her feelings changed and she thought yours had too. She believed in love, believed she was loveable. Is that so wrong?' The anger was muted now, and he could see a shadow in her blue eyes, a sadness on her face, and he wanted to reach out and smooth it away.

'No.' He shook his head. 'It wasn't wrong.

But she should have told me. That way, perhaps I could at least have stopped the whole misconception early. I won't change—I don't understand feelings, so I don't want love or commitment, but I don't want to hurt anyone either. That was never my intention. I thought being upfront meant I had it covered. I didn't.'

'Maybe you can't always have it covered,' she said, and now he heard a sadness in her voice. 'But I appreciate that you tried, that you try to minimise the risk of hurting someone by keeping it short-term and being honest. I am sorry for Ruby, but I do see you didn't lead her on.'

He sensed that she thinking of something in her own past, perhaps a past relationship.

'Thank you for telling me your side, and I'm sorry. I shouldn't have judged you based on a tabloid article. Shouldn't have disapproved of your lifestyle without understanding your motivations.'

The apology disarmed him; the idea someone had listened to him and come back with a positive judgment warmed him. He smiled at her; she smiled back and the impact jolted him. She looked so god damned beautiful with the sunlight glinting blonde highlights into her glossy brown hair, dappling the strands in sunlight. Her eyes sparkled, luminous, and he wished it all wasn't so complicated; he wished that he didn't have so much baggage and that he could be one of those people who understood love and commitment.

He shook his head to dislodge the absurdity of the thought, self-aware enough to know that it was generated by the unfamiliar warmth of approval and understanding. Reminded himself that he did not need validation from anyone except himself. This wasn't about validation. It was about maximising spin so that they could both protect their business reputations.

'Thank you for listening,' he said. 'And I do understand your concerns. If we go ahead with this, when we break up you can be the instigator. You will not be seen as a discarded girlfriend, I promise. For now, I suggest we go on the offensive—embrace the publicity, stress that it is early days but that we are serious, though right now our focus is on the fundraiser. We can use the publicity to promote the charity then, once the fundraiser is over, our relationship can become long distance, media interest should die down and we can fizzle out. How does that sound?'

Lily hesitated. 'That sounds…as though it

could work.' She clenched her hands into fists. 'It has to.'

'Agreed.'

'So what next?' she asked.

'We should move out of the hotel. I suggest we stay in the villa—it will be easier to avoid undue press attention. I'll sort out a cleaning team now to blitz the place. That way, we can move in later today.'

She nodded. 'OK. I'd better call my mum. Before we go public, I'll try our story out on her.'

CHAPTER EIGHT

As Lily listened to the buzz of the phone, nerves strummed through her, along with a disbelief that she had agreed to this. On some level it sounded utterly bonkers, but somehow Darius had made it sound possible, believable, and a sudden unexpected frisson ran through her, along with a determination to make it work.

'Lily?' Her mum's voice was sharp. 'What's the update?'

'I didn't tell you before, I didn't tell anyone before, but Darius and I have been seeing each other. Lady Fairley-Godfrey introduced us, and when she couldn't come across to Morocco she suggested we work together. We wanted to keep it under the radar, because we didn't want any press intrusion, but obviously it's a bit late for that now.'

Lily came to a stop and held her breath, wondering if her mum would buy it, and wondering if she even wanted her to. Because telling her mum that she was dating a millionaire... That was *embarrassing*. She was doing the exact thing her mother had advised her to do and she could almost hear her mum's brain whirring and calculating.

'Hmm.' Maria's voice was thoughtful. 'Well... I hadn't expected that. I thought he kissed you because he was a bit bored and you were there and available.'

Lily gritted her teeth, wondering if there was any truth in that. She tried to recall Darius's words, telling her the attraction was real and mutual. 'Out of interest, why did you think I kissed him?'

'Because the man is drop-dead gorgeous and you couldn't help yourself.' *Fair point*. 'But this changes things. I know you don't agree with my attitude to men, but please, for once just listen. Darius is dating you for a reason— most likely it's the novelty factor. So use this opportunity. Make the most of it. Get publicity for your business, get gifts, get *something*...'

Lily opened her mouth and closed it again. Her mother was suggesting a deal, and in truth that was exactly what this relationship was: a deal, like all her mother's relationships. Especially the one with her father, whoever he was. Lily pushed the question away; she'd accepted that her mother did not want to disclose the information; that no amount of cajoling, begging, shouting and reasoning would change her mind. Her mother had made a deal and, to give Maria her due, she kept her side of any bargain she made.

Like Darius did with his relationships. The idea, the similarities, made her edgy. Lily took a deep breath. She and Darius might have made a deal but it was not equivalent to what her mother had done. This relationship with a millionaire was strictly on paper only and, once it was over, she would tell Maria the truth.

But for now, she said, 'Mum, it's really early days. I just wanted to let you know what's going on.'

'Early days may be all you have. Make sure you get something from him.'

'I don't need anything from him. I earn my own money, good money. I have a business and a job I love.'

There was a silence and she felt the familiar frustration that her mum didn't get it; that she didn't understand Lily at all. The gulf between them was so wide she wondered if it would ever be possible to bridge it. If perhaps one day her mother would profess pride in Lily's achievements. The hope became more forlorn with each passing day.

But, all that aside, her mother was an expert on wealthy men and how to lure them in; if she had suggested that Darius had kissed her because he was bored or for the novelty factor, she was probably spot-on.

The idea was unwelcome, and Lily glanced at him, further irritated by how god damned gorgeous he was, standing in the Moroccan sunshine, phone to his ear. Her face creased into a scowl. As if sensing her scrutiny, he turned and studied her expression and then to her intense surprise he pulled a funny face. A genuine, slapstick-comedy screwing up of his features, along with a waggle of first one eyebrow than another. She couldn't help it; she smiled, the scowl chased away.

And he smiled back, a real humdinger of a smile that lit and creased his grey eyes. And now desire hummed inside her and she couldn't help but focus on the strength of his features, the shifting colours in his grey eyes, the line of his jaw and the shape of his lips. How could he make her feel like this without so much as touching her?

She didn't know, and suddenly she didn't care, recalling his voice, the way he'd looked at her when he'd told her that what they had was 'the real thing'. Maybe it didn't matter if that was generated by the novelty factor; hell, this was completely novel for her too. Nothing had prepared her for this; her body had taken on a life of its own, the common-sense part of her brain shut down by the sheer intensity of desire.

What had her mum said? To make the most of the opportunity. Her mother had meant in terms of monetary gain; well, maybe there was another way to look at it. She was stuck with this fake relationship, but she had a choice—to see it as a penance or an opportunity.

Right now, she wasn't sure exactly what that meant, but a shiver of anticipation skittered through her as he dropped his phone into his pocket and headed towards her.

'All sorted,' he said. 'Cleaners are going in to blitz the villa right now. I've also put some feelers out for a potential band.'

'Perfect. That frees us up to go shopping,' She must not forget that they were here to or-ganise a fundraiser as well as faking a rela-tionship. 'There is also a chance we will be recognised or snapped, so we need to look con-vincing at all times. Do you think we should hold hands?'

There was a pause and she sensed his reluctance, and on some level she understood it. Holding hands did denote a sense of intimacy, a connection. She'd loved holding Tom's hand, having seen it as visible proof they were together. Once he'd met Cynthia, that was one of the first things he'd stopped, telling her she was being too clingy. A sign she should have read.

'Or maybe that's a bad idea,' she said.

'No, it's not. It's a good idea. Holding hands is exactly what we should do. It's an important detail, it's what real couples do.' He held out his hand and she looked at it, at its strength and the strong shape of his fingers. 'Let's start now.'

Darius told himself to get a grip—literally. He grasped her hand and felt something…a tug, a connection…as though there was a significance to the gesture. He told himself it was just the unfamiliarity. Darius didn't hold hands, to him that was something only real couples did. The thought made him edgy and he saw Lily glance at him, then down at their entwined fingers, and he sensed her reluctance matched his own.

Telling himself he was being ridiculous, he gently tightened his hold. This was a show, a pretence… Things were complicated enough without him over-thinking a simple gesture like this.

They started walking, and as they made their way through the labyrinth of alleyways he gradually relaxed and absorbed the atmosphere, the environment, the cobbled streets, vibrant colours, the noise and the bustle.

'I am really looking forward to this,' she said. 'I did some research and the whole history of the souks is fascinating.'

'Tell me,' he said.

'You sure?' She looked surprised. 'You don't have to be polite.'

'I'm not. I want to know—knowing the history of a place makes it come alive, means you can picture how it became what it is today. A bit like people—your past shapes you, just like this place is shaped by its past.'

'OK, but stop me if I get boring.'

Looking down at her animated expression, it occurred to him that Lily was many things but boring was definitely not one of them. She tucked a tendril of hair behind her ear and started to speak,

'The souks, or trading places, all started when Marrakesh was founded in 1070, so centuries and centuries ago. Gold, ivory, metalwork…all were traded.'

As she spoke, he could see the picture she painted of laden camels crossing the desert carrying exotic goods over miles of sand, carrying news of different places and adventures.

'The city was founded by Aku Babr, who built the original gates of Marrakesh. Over the next hundred years or so the walls were built and they are roughly the same design as they are now. How incredible is that? All those years ago that basic heritage, the core trading belief, started and still lives on, and today we're part of that.'

She came to a stop at the entrance to the sprawling maze of stalls and gave a half-embarrassed smile. 'Sorry. I told you to stop me if I went on and on.'

'You told me to stop you if I got bored. I'm not…' He took her other hand in his. 'I promise.'

Their gazes meshed and all he wanted to do was pull her closer and kiss her again, wondering if she wanted him to, wondering if he should, and then the moment was gone as the crowds jostled into them, breaking them apart.

Lily opened her bag. 'I have a list of things to buy, and a map. The souks are split by types of goods on sale and I've read up on the best way to bargain.'

They stepped forward and she gave a gasp at

the sprawl of goods on offer, the vibrant cacophony of smells, noise and colours that assaulted their senses. 'Look,' she said with delight as she pointed to the row of stalls. 'I wonder if I'll ever be able to buy olives from the supermarket again.'

He could see her point as they both surveyed the mounds of glistening, plump green olives, small, wrinkly black ones and others that were a luscious purple-red, all flanked by bright-yellow lemons that filled the air with a citrus tang, overlaid with the spicy burst from piles of bright-red and dark-green chillies. Behind the fresh produce were shelves covered in columns of jars filled to the brim with a variety pickles, olives, lemons and oils.

Lily gestured to the olives. 'I'd like to buy a few to sample. I am going to put snacks in the guests' rooms and in the lounge.'

Ten minutes later, they had purchased a variety of fresh olives and she pulled out a notebook from her bag. 'I'll jot some tasting notes down.'

'In which case, you don't want to get oil on the book. Here.' He headed into a slightly less crowded bit of the souk and they stopped. He took an olive. 'Here you go,'

She hesitated then opened her mouth and he

popped the olive in, felt an instant frisson as his finger brushed the softness of her lips and heard her intake of breath before she slightly stepped back, her eyes wide as she met his gaze. It was almost as if the crowds faded away, as if it were just the two of them.

Then she blinked and looked down almost absently at the notebook. 'Um…that was amazing, strong and full of flavour, and…'

He bit into one himself. 'And leaves you wanting more,' he said, and she caught her breath.

'Yes, it does. Could I try another, please?'

Her lips parted, his gaze fixed on them and he reached out and, oh, so gently rubbed a finger over them. 'I'm removing the oil,' he said, his voice husky. 'So it doesn't impede the taste of the next one.'

He dropped his hand and she looked at him, taking a step closer, and now she reached up and slid her finger over his lip, and he held his breath as sensation rocketed through him, clenching his gut with a need he saw mirrored in her eyes.

'Good idea,' she said softly.

'I'm ready.' Eyes on her, he put another olive into her mouth and then one into his own.

'This one is saltier,' she said. 'Followed by a tang of spice.'

'Chilli oil,' he said. 'It adds the spice. The salt causes a build-up of taste, of sensation, and then the heat.'

The only thing that rescued them again was the jostle of the crowds.

'I… We'd better move on,' she said.

CHAPTER NINE

As THEY WALKED Lily tried to pull her scattered senses into order—what had happened there? How could such a small gesture unleash such a sensual torrent of desire inside her?

Deep breath. She had to focus on the job in hand. Had to focus on looking around her, absorbing the sheer chaos of the atmosphere: the strident voices of the tradespeople; the good-natured bargaining and expressive hand gestures; the smiles when a deal was made. They walked along the cobbled street of another souk, this one covered with an iron trellis and crowded with tourists all examining the wares, textiles, jewellery and furniture.

But, despite all her efforts, she was also so aware of Darius that the sights and smells around her seemed slightly muted against the backdrop of sensations running through her and the tingle of her lips where he'd touched them.

Focus. She came to a stop as they entered

another souk and this image did at least break through as she surveyed the row after row of pointy-toed Moroccan slippers in every imaginable colour and design in seemingly endless numbers.

'We need these,' she declared, and he looked down at her, raising his eyebrows in question.

'For the guests,' she said. 'They can wear them inside then take them away with them at the end.'

The conversation at least tracked her back some way to normalcy as they continued their journey. They stopped at the apothecary stalls where she gazed at the exotic offerings: scorpions, medicinal leeches, snails whose slime could help with wrinkles and various ingredients to mix anything, from love spells to things more sinister.

They arrived at the stalls she'd been looking for. 'Here,' she said. 'This is what I wanted—black Moroccan soap.' Picking up a sample, she inhaled the earthy, cleansing smell then passed it to him.

As he smelt it, she had an overwhelming image of rubbing it onto him, rinsing it off and then inhaling the scent from his skin. She closed her eyes, wondering if she was getting a fever.

'I like it,' he said, his voice a rumble. She nodded and slipped her hand into his as they continued to wander the souks, stopping at different food stalls. They sampled *msemen*: a flaky flatbread filled with cheese; *pastille*: filo pastry parcels dusted with sugar but filled with delicious savoury fillings; all washed down with mint tea. Then his phone beeped and he looked down.

'The villa is done,' he said.

'Then let's head back.'

As they walked and hailed a taxi, she tried to distract herself tried to focus on lists, on the villa, on everything that she needed to think about over the coming days, but to no avail.

In the end it was a relief to approach the vast villa and watch Darius pull out the keys.

'You were right,' he said softly. 'There is a knack to the door. Let me show you.' He demonstrated and she tried to focus on his hands, how they twisted and turned. 'You turn and jiggle at the same time,' he said. 'Have a go.'

She stepped next to him and could smell the soap he used, a fresh, work-like smell— coal tar, perhaps. She tried to turn the key but couldn't, her fingers all fumble and thumbs. He stood behind her and placed his hands over hers, gently turning and uplifting them. Lily tried to concentrate, she really did, but all she could feel was the strength of his body behind her and she couldn't help but accidentally lean back, heard his sharp intake of breath, then the door was open and they walked in.

The fresh scent of furniture polish and clean, fresh citrus assailed her nostrils and she took in the shine of the floor, the cobweb-free walls and ceilings, the fresh gleam of the door handles, and headed into the lounge. The leather sofas had been cleaned and looked both stylish and comfortable, as did the eclectic arm chairs that she could now see were a deep-red colour. Tapestries hung from the walls and there were low glass tables strategically placed for drinks and food.

The smells and sights acted like a welcome wake-up call, a reminder she was here to work, and she turned to Darius with a smile. 'They have done an incredible job in here. I wouldn't have recognised it from yesterday.'

They walked across the corridor to the kitchen and she noted with approval that here too everything shone, and there was a lingering undertone of disinfectant that indicated the clean had been deep.

'When did you buy the villa?' she asked.

'About a year ago,' he said. 'I bought it on a

whim and since then I haven't had time to get back, or decide what to do with it.' He walked over to the fridge, pulled it open and checked the temperature. He took the olives out of the backpack and stored them inside. 'Perhaps now that it's up and running I can use it as a B&B. Give the profits to the charity.'

She glanced at him and realised another of her preconceptions about this man had been knocked away. His idea was a far cry from her assumption he'd bought it in order to throw lavish parties or entertain his celebrity girlfriends.

'Let's go and look upstairs,' he said.

Every bedroom sparkled, the bed posts had been polished, the marble floors were dust-free and the rugs looked freshly vacuumed. The bathrooms gleamed too, and Lily nodded approval, even as a sudden worry assailed her.

'I didn't expect this level of cleaning—I was planning on doing some of it. I'll reduce my fee to compensate. I don't want the fundraiser to lose money.'

'It won't. I agreed as my donation to the fund that I would donate the villa and any associated costs in getting it event-ready. This doesn't impact the money the fundraiser will make. You don't have the time to get the villa up to scratch on your own and help arrange the fundraiser.

You would have had to get help in anyway, and that is partly my fault. I thought the villa was in slightly better shape than it actually was.'

Damn it—it turned out that Darius Kingsleigh really was not the man she'd believed him to be at all. He wasn't the Lothario callously leaving a scatter of broken hearts in his wake. He wasn't an idler. He was a man willing to help others with his money and his time.

And the knowledge gave her a sudden sense of warmth, even as she recognised the ramifications, the danger. One of the main reasons to hold attraction at bay had been the fact that Darius was the wrong sort of man and had the wrong sort of character. What if he wasn't? What then? It was a question she didn't know the answer to.

Seeing that he was looking at her with a question in his eyes, she tried to think and fight the urge to move over, to brush her lips against his and pull him into one of the bedrooms...

Her mind somehow scrambled back into gear. This man was paying her wages; their relationship was a fake one. 'That is very generous of you,' she said, knowing her voice sounded clipped, but it was the only way to rein herself in. 'I'd better get to work. I'll go round and inventory what else we need to buy.'

'Fine. I need to make a few calls about the

band, and also about some form of security for the night as well. And release our statement, explaining our relationship status.'

His tone was all business, in line with her own, and she wasn't sure if she was glad or sad. She knew there was a part of her that wanted him to feel the same way that she did, wanted him to be as tempted, as swirled up inside.

'Sounds good,' she managed. 'Good luck with the calls.'

Darius dropped his phone back into his pocket, walked over to the open window and allowed the early-evening breeze to waft over him in the vain hope it might cool him down. He wasn't sure what was going on any more, or whether he was coming or going. The time with Lily seemed to have done something to his head: wandering hand in hand through the souks, discussing slippers, feeding each other olives... The hours had taken on a dream-like quality, a sense of an alternative reality in which he was the sort of man who did things like that.

But he wasn't, and he had to remember this was all make-believe—an alternative reality that did not and could not exist.

He turned and headed to find Lily, eventually running her to earth in a small study, sitting at a desk, her head bent over a notebook. She looked up as he entered.

'Hey,' she said.

'Hey,' he said. 'I came to give you a progress report and run something past you.'

'Go ahead,' she said, putting her pencil down.

'I may have found a band. A band that plays *gnawa*—traditional Moroccan music that dates back to the eleventh century.'

Her face scrunched in a frown as she searched her memory banks. 'I don't think I've heard of it.'

'It was brought to Morocco from further in Africa by slaves, and back then it was played in secret ceremonies—the music helped ease the suffering and created a kind of community, something that bonded the different people. The music has continued and many believe it has influenced the blues, jazz…you name it. Scores of famous musicians have incorporated the traditions and styles. The band I've found have agreed in principle to come to the event, but they have asked us to attend a venue tonight. They are playing at one of Marrakesh's top restaurants, so the idea is we go for dinner and listen to the band.'

'That sounds like a great idea…' She broke off and looked at him and he could almost see the penny drop. 'I assume the press will be there—so this will be our first public outing as a couple.'

'Yes. I tipped the press off. It's one of Marrakesh's top restaurants, a haunt of the rich and famous, the band is up and coming so it seemed like a good place and occasion for our first public outing.' He could see a touch of anxiety cross her blue eyes.

'Do you think we're ready to go on show?'

'Yes,' he said simply.

'That's easy for you, you're used to it,' she said. 'I'm not. Any tips you want to share?'

'For me, I've always tried to be in control of publicity as much as I can—tried to use it to my advantage. A lot of my celebrity dates were trying to promote movies, so we'd use the publicity for that. Recently, I've focused all interviews and articles on my business. So focus on why the publicity is good for you, rather than it being nerve-racking or anxiety-making. You are doing this for your business and to promote a good cause—the fundraiser and the charity behind it.'

She rose to her feet, walked over to the window then turned back to him.

'But that also means if I mess up the stakes are higher.'

'You'll be fine. Just don't drop your guard or forget the part you're playing, and remember that a whole lot of it is true. You are a professional, successful woman; you are in Morocco to organise a fundraiser; you were given the job by Gemma, and she did ask us to organise it together.'

'Yes. But I am *not* dating you.' The words were said with emphasis.

'No.' Though in that moment he wondered why not, what was stopping them. He imagined dating Lily, walking hand in hand, being able to give in to the attraction, laughing, talking...

He shook his head. Despite the pretence, he was the client; more than that, he didn't know how to date someone like Lily. What rules would he put in place? He didn't even know her relationship history, or her wishes for the future. 'We're not dating but the attraction is real.'

'So what do you suggest—I plaster myself all over you? Again.' The sarcasm was clear.

'That's not what I meant.' He tried to blink away the image of her doing just that, recalling the press of her body against his, the closeness of her.

'What do you mean?'

'We just need to show it exists so, when we look at each other, remember our kiss.'

Her eyes widened. 'Are you sure that will work?'

'Yes.' He shrugged. 'OK, no, I'm not sure. I've never tried to fake an attraction that is real. Why don't we try it?'

He reached out and took both her hands in his so they were facing each other, the breeze from the open window enveloping them in the gentle floral smells of the bursts of flowers in the courtyard below.

Suddenly Darius wasn't sure how good an idea this was as the atmosphere shifted a notch and an image of their kiss imploded in his brain. Heat climbed the slant of her cheekbones and her eyes darkened, lingering on his lips, and his gut clenched as he recalled the magic that had happened when his lips had touched hers. Now they were leaning towards each other, her eyes lit with a need that he knew mirrored his own.

The need was as irresistible as it was inevitable and now their lips met and he was lost in the sensations it evoked—he could taste mint tea, smell her light floral scent and a lingering sense of sunshine and black soap. Liquid desire pooled in his gut as he deepened the kiss, hearing her soft moan of desire, her fingers tangling in his hair, and he was lost.

Until finally they pulled back. 'I...' Lily stared at him, her hair dishevelled, her face flushed. Damn it; she looked so beautiful, his heart skipped.

'I'm sorry,' he said, then shook his head. 'No, I'm not sorry. I know I should be, and truly, I didn't intend that to happen. But I can't be sorry. It was...'

'Magical,' she said softly. 'But you're right. We shouldn't have done it.'

No, they shouldn't have. Because this couldn't go anywhere. The rules were in place. It was a pretend relationship, a fake. Messing it up could impact his business and hers, and he was already out of his depth, aware that this was different from his previous forays into arranged relationships. Before, he'd always been in control from the start. Now, the last thing he felt was in control, and it had to stop.

'No,' he agreed, but somehow the simple syllable was hard to formulate.

'I'll go and get ready,' Lily said. 'I'll meet you downstairs in about an hour, if that works time-wise.'

'Sure.' It was all he could get himself together to say.

CHAPTER TEN

LILY STARED AT the clothes in her suitcase, trying to focus on what she should wear for this fake date, but she couldn't think straight. Her whole being was consumed by that kiss. Darius was right—she couldn't feel regret, even though she knew they shouldn't have done it, it was increasingly hard for her to work out why. Because right now all she wanted was him.

Come on, Lily. The man was paying her—he was the *client.* That mattered.

Huh, said a little voice. *The whole world believes you're sleeping with him, so who cares?*

The answer to that should have been obvious: she did. But in the giddy aftermath of that kiss she didn't. And that was a problem in itself. It showed she was letting attraction mess with her professionalism, her integrity.

She dug her nails into the palms of her hands and forced herself to concentrate, pulling out a simple grey dress that should denote 'professional' and 'understated'. Which was good. After all, if everyone was going to believe this relationship was based on novelty factor, then there was no point Lily trying to compete with Darius's past flings. She didn't even want to; she didn't need to.

Because the attraction was real; she knew that now. She had felt the urgency of his need and known it matched her own, had seen the desire blaze from his eyes, a desire that had heated her skin and clenched her insides. As she looked at herself, it almost felt transformative. Her dark-blue eyes sparkled, her skin seemed translucent and the simple grey dress seemed to shimmer.

That was it—she felt as if she were shimmering. Felt as if she were a different Lily.

She had never felt this way before. She'd believed Tom to be 'the one' but she had never once shimmered in his presence, never been so consumed with a need to touch and be touched this strong. A sneaking thought slipped into the recesses of her mind. Maybe this was how short-term relationships worked—they were all about attraction, all about the physical, about living in the moment because there was no future and that was OK. In fact that was the point.

Shaking the thoughts away, she applied the

minimum of make-up, a swipe of mascara and a hint of lip gloss, and rose, feeling absurdly shy as she descended the sweeping staircase and entered the lounge.

She entered the room and again desire impacted her at the sight of him. Dressed in a dark-grey suit over a dark shirt, no tie, his dark hair slightly damp and curling against his neck he took her breath away.

'Looking good,' she said, her voice sounding shaky, the words not ones she would usually have used.

'Right back atcha,' he said, pointing both fingers at her in an exaggerated movement. Then he said, 'I don't know why I did that,' and they both looked at each other and simultaneously burst into laughter.

'Let's go,' he said. 'We can walk there—it's about half an hour—or I can call a cab.'

'Let's walk.' That way she could revel in holding his hand, and in the sheer proximity of him.

And she did, savouring every stride through the maze of alleys in the cooling dusk air. There was no need for conversation; the after-effect of the kiss seemed to have robbed them of coherence and allowed them simply to be together.

As they approached the venue, she slowed to take in the hotel's magnificence. Rose-tinted stone walls rose in a splendour of turrets in a mosaic courtyard dotted with palm trees of varying size and width, all magically illuminated to give the whole a sense of a fairy tale. 'It's beautiful...' She breathed as they walked forward and then she became aware of the people at the entrance who turned at their arrival, cameras in hand.

Her steps faltered, but then his hand tightened round hers, offering reassurance. She walked forward, imagining that this was a photo shoot for an article promoting her business, and she smiled her coolest, most business-like smile, one that mixed friendliness with professionalism as they mounted the wide sweep of the stairs that led inside, to a lobby that had to be seen to be believed, and she didn't know where to look first.

There were glittering chandeliers suspended from a frescoed ceiling above immense, plush velvet sofas flanked by plasterwork detailed with arabesques and motifs, along which were pillars and alcoves with art deco lights and flowers arranged in bright vases, beneath which a gleaming polished marble floor stretched as far as the eye could see.

'Mr Kingsleigh, Ms Culpepper—welcome. Let me take you to the restaurant, one of the four we are proud to harbour under our roof.'

'Thank you,'

They followed their guide through plushly decorated rooms, past intricate mosaic pillars and verdant greenery, the air scented with orange blossoms. They reached an arched doorway leading to a patio restaurant set on a courtyard that seemed enchanted. The floor was laid with mosaic tiles in earthy brown-and-red designs. Massive candles and lights illuminated pools and fountains. The tables were separated by arched trellises of flowers and leaves.

'This way, please.'

They were seated at an intimate, beautifully laid table covered with small platters of pastries and olives, and a waiter materialised to hand them heavy, tasselled menus.

'I will be back for your orders shortly,' he said.

Lily started to read. 'This all looks amazing.'

'Why don't we order a selection of items and share?'

'Good idea,'

They ordered *briouates*—pastries filled with meat or fish and cheese and lemon—served with a coriander sauce, along with Berber-style lamb tagine and a chicken couscous dish.

As the waiter walked away, a man and a woman rose from their seats and headed towards them. Darius frowned and turned to Lily. 'Business colleagues—high-powered couple Rob and Belinda Keating,' he murmured.

Lily felt a flutter of anxiety as she studied the couple. The man wasn't tall but he carried an aura of wealth, and the woman exuded confidence, her dress screaming 'designer'. Like Lily's mum, she walked with a knowledge that on her a bin bag would have looked 'designer'. The woman met her gaze and Lily saw curiosity in her green eyes. She was sure this beautiful woman was wondering what Darius was doing with Lily.

Doubt, and a memory of her stepsisters mocking her looks, mocking her intelligence, putting her down, came through her like a tsunami.

Then Darius's hand covered hers in a brief, reassuring grasp and he smiled at her, a smile full of solidarity. 'We've got this,' he said in an undertone, and the stress on the 'we' in his words gave her a much-needed jolt of confidence, reminding her they were in this together.

For their professional reputations, she wouldn't let herself or Darius down.

The couple arrived at the table and Darius rose, stepping round the table to stand by her side, the bulk of his body an extra reassurance. It seemed natural to step slightly closer to him so she could catch the scent of the black soap, an added reminder of a sense of intimacy.

'Hi, Rob. Hi, Belinda. This is Lily Culpepper.'

'It's lovely to meet you, Lily. We are stakeholders in YourChoiceBookings, and of course we are also friends of Darius.'

'It's good to meet you too,' Lily said, shaking hands and smiling, aware of an undercurrent between the two men.

Rob gave a genial smile. 'Well, Lily, you make sure that you aren't keeping Darius from his duties in the boardroom. We'd rather see him gracing the columns in the *Financial Times* than the gossip pages and social media.'

Lily forced herself not to narrow her eyes and looked up at Darius with a smile before turning a cooler smile on Rob. 'You've no need to worry about that. I don't think *anyone* could keep Darius out of the boardroom. And I wouldn't want to even if I could—I have a pretty heavy workload myself. That's why I am so glad of this opportunity to mix business and pleasure: we're organising a fundraiser together for Lady Gemma.'

'Such a wonderful woman,' Belinda cooed.

'And, believe me, we tried incredibly hard to avoid the gossip columns. But…' Lily shrugged. 'Unfortunately, that ship has sailed.'

'But we're planning to focus publicity on the fundraiser,' Darius said. 'In fact, as you're in Morocco, I could ask Gemma to add you to the guest list.'

'That would be marvellous,' Belinda said instantly. 'You're both angels. And now we'll leave you two lovebirds to it. You both look very happy together and so in tune.'

Lily sat back down just as the waiter arrived with their food.

'Phew,' she said. 'That felt like a bit of a grilling.'

'It was,' Darius said. 'Bob is an important stakeholder and a good friend, but he's a businessman first and foremost. He gave me a chance and…well… He agrees with my policy of keeping my personal life out of the papers. So that photo would have rattled him.'

They spent a few minutes admiring the food. The presentation was flawless, the vegetables of the tagine artistically arranged to completely cover the spiced meat below.

Once they had tasted everything, Lily looked across at Darius. 'Is that why you haven't had a personal life since Ruby?' she asked.

'Partly. Though in all honesty I haven't really had time, or inclination. Work has taken complete precedence and I've enjoyed every single minute.'

Curiosity touched her; she could hear the sincerity in his voice and now she questioned her blithe assumption that he was some sort of figurehead, or had been handed a business opportunity on a silver platter. 'Tell me about your company.'

'It's a booking company—a place where people can choose and book their stay somewhere, or an event venue, but the amount of detail I programmed into the system means they can really tailor their stay to them.'

'Did you do the programming?'

'Yes, I did all of it. I got the idea years ago, partly because of all the different jobs I worked at the Kingsleigh empire.' His voice was neutral but Lily was sure a shadow crossed his eyes. 'I did every job going, from porter to cleaner to receptionist, and it gave me a true insight into the detail of the hotel business.

'It got me thinking. I spoke to so many guests who loved certain things that others weren't bothered about. I spoke to one woman who loved the luxury touches, and another who went online and said she could easily bring luxuries with her. People with bad backs who wanted guaranteed comfort—soft beds rather than hard. Some people liked spending time in the room, others wanted to use it as a base. Working people versus tourists...'

He broke off. 'Sorry—I could go on for ever. The one common factor was people didn't want to trawl through lots of reviews to find out if a particular hotel suited them. So I came up with an idea and applied my computer geekiness to it.'

'You're a computer geek?'

He grinned and lifted a finger to his lips. 'It's a well-kept secret. Don't tell anyone. I have re-packaged myself as a programming expert—it sounds better.'

'But really you were a high-school geek.'

The smile hardened slightly. 'It was a bit of a secret hobby. Geekiness didn't go with the Kingsleigh image.' Lily heard the faint hint of bitterness under the light-hearted tone. 'But by the time I was a teenager I could have hacked into pretty much any system, and I was fairly expert at programming and coding, so I was able to put everything together and the idea for YourChoiceBookings was born. Then it was all about research, testing, hoping and tweaking until I had it right.'

Lily nodded. 'Then it's the even scarier bit,' she said. 'When I decided to set up Culpepper's, it took me a while to get ready. I had to save up the capital, find the right premises, work out how the staffing would work, what about advertising... I made so many colour-coded plans, so many spreadsheets. That was hard work, but it wasn't scary. What was scary was actually putting the plan into action.'

'All the hopes and fears—the hope you'll realise your dream, prove yourself. The fear you won't, that you've got it wrong, or you can't do it.'

'That's exactly it.'

She'd wanted to succeed so badly to show her mother that there was a different way to make money—that a person could have a career, that looks weren't everything. She'd wanted to show her stepsisters that they had been wrong—that she'd survived their bullying and it had made her stronger. Show them that she wasn't the failure they'd taunted her with being. She'd wanted to show the world that she could stand on her own two feet and that she was worth something.

And she could hear from Darius's voice that he had felt the same. She wondered what he had had to prove, and to whom he was proving it.

He smiled at her and raised his glass of wine. 'To our companies and our success,' he said.

'I'll drink to that.' They clinked glasses and the sound of crystal on crystal seemed to symbolise something—perhaps a common understanding, a connection between them.

Stop, Lily. Remember, this is all an illusion. She and Darius inhabited different worlds.

'Though I'm not trying to compare Culpepper's to YourChoiceBookings. You are a multimillion turnover global player. I'm not.'

'That doesn't matter.' His voice was resonant with sincerity, the depth tingling over her skin. 'Turnover doesn't matter. Culpepper's is your achievement, your idea, and you built it. You rode that roller coaster of taking an idea and believing you could make it work whilst simultaneously fighting the fear that it won't. You put in the grit, the hours and had the worries, financial and personal. That's what matters.'

'Yes, it does. Though it must be nice feeling your company was a family venture, part of an empire—I remember sometimes feeling really alone.'

'I get…' Darius broke off, his expression unreadable, and she wondered what he had been about to say. That he got that? But he couldn't. She truly believed he felt the same pride in his company that she did in hers and that he deserved to feel that pride. But he hadn't been alone; he had had untold wealth and family connections behind him.

'What you mean,' he finished. 'But the most important thing is having a vision. I had a vision and I needed to follow it through to the end, one way or the other.'

His voice was hard, full of steel determination, and again she sensed that whatever his status, whatever his family wealth, his need for success was as absolute as her own.

She studied his face, the strength of his features, the shifting colours in his grey eyes, the line of his jaw and the shape of his lips. Felt that little clutch of desire in her tummy again. His gaze met hers straight-on, and now he returned the scrutiny and she saw the steel in his eyes morph into desire. Had to resist an urge to wriggle in her seat and instead forced herself to lift her glass.

'To our visions,' she said, and again they clinked glasses.

'So what other visions do you have?' he asked. His voice was low, and seemed to hum over her. 'Apart from for your business. What do you want?'

You. The word nearly slipped out and she swallowed it down, even as she recognised its truth. She wanted him with a depth of desire she hadn't believed possible, and she wanted to do something about it, but fear held her back. Fear of rejection, fear of getting in over her head. Also a fear that she would regret it—regret the loss of integrity and professionalism.

And of course there was the ever-constant fear that she wouldn't measure up—those old insecurities resurfaced. It was safer to be alone; being with someone was a guaranteed way to heartbreak and pain. She knew that—she knew love was temporary, a shifting chimera, an illusion.

He studied her expression 'So what's your answer? What else is important to you, apart from work? What do you do for fun?'

Lily thought back over the past two years, since her split from Tom. 'Fun has been in short supply,' she said. 'I suppose work has consumed me. What about you? When's the last time you had fun?'

'Honestly?' he asked, and his smile was suddenly rueful...slightly crooked.

'Yes.'

'Here, with you. I've had fun.'

So had she, she realised: exploring the square, walking through the souks, tasting olives, choosing soap, admiring the slippers... It had all been fun.

'So have I,' she said softly, feeling absurdly shy. Looking away, she saw that the band was tuning up. A makeshift dance area had been cleared and many people had turned their chairs to face the group of men on the stage. She tried to remind herself why they were here.

'Hopefully the band are going to be right for the fundraiser,' she said, pulling out a notebook and pen from her evening bag. 'I'll take some notes.'

'Good idea. Then I have another way of assessing them.'

'Yes?'

His voice was deep, with a soupçon of amusement, a teasing note that seemed to caress her. 'Would you do me the honour of dancing with me?'

Lily tried to imagine what dancing with Darius would be like: to be allowed to be up close, to touch. 'I...'

'Actually, I don't care about assessment, I *want* to dance with you.'

As their gazes locked, all the earlier fears dissipated, dissolving under the fierce flame of desire burning dark in the grey depths of his eyes. This was real, and held a power that made her anxieties and scruples irrelevant.

'I want to dance with you too,' she said, and now anticipation swirled in her tummy as she forced herself to turn away from him, to watch as the lead singer took the mic and started to introduce the band.

CHAPTER ELEVEN

DARIUS WATCHED AS Lily's pencil skimmed over her notebook, focusing as much as he could on the words from the stage, facts that would normally have held his undivided interest. The man explained that he was a *maalem*, the lead singer, but so much more.

'To me, being a *maalem* is a way of life, an embodiment of musical and spiritual traditions and history, but also of music and meanings today. A fusion of past and present, a way of honouring both.'

Lily's face was serious now. She turned and met Darius's gaze and he knew that the *maalem*'s words resonated with her; that she understood that this man was more than a lead singer; that this was a man who had dedicated his life to his art, to his work.

The *maalem* went on briefly to describe the instruments the band would use: the *gimbri*, a three-string lute that he would play; castanets, known as *qraqeb* or *karkabas*; and double-headed drums called *tbels*, which were played with one curved and one straight stick.

'Now we will begin. We will start with some of the more traditional songs and then move on to the more modern.'

Lily turned to Darius.

'It is like we said yesterday—the past shapes the future.'

'But sometimes it is important to live in the present.'

'And to enjoy the moment,' she said. 'Maybe we've both been so caught up in work, the need to succeed, that we haven't been doing that.'

The music started and for the next ten minutes they sat transfixed along with the rest of the audience. The performers were dressed in traditional electric-blue robes and brightly coloured fezzes, and the sheer synchronicity of their movements, all somehow orchestrated by the *maalem* as he played the lute, was as hypnotic as the music itself. The twists and turns of the swaying dancers as they shook the heavy iron castanets seemed to shake beats of movement and sound into the air, with pulsating speed alongside the bass, transcendental notes of the lute and the thrum of the drums.

The words themselves were in Arabic, and they seemed to call to something in Darius, to urge exactly what Lily had said—to enjoy the moment, to seize it, take it and feel the joy of living despite, or perhaps because, life also contained pain and suffering.

And she must have felt the same, because now she rose and held out her hand to him. He took it and they headed towards the stage. Once there, he felt as though they were one, standing oh, so close but without touching, their movements in perfect synch and harmony as they moved to the music.

He was consumed by her closeness. She was so tantalisingly near that the need to touch, to feel her body against him, was excruciating, almost hurt, and yet it heightened the sense of anticipation as the beat of the music seemed to grip them in its spell.

And then the music segued into something else, into a blues rhythm, and now they both moved forward. He heard her sigh of relief when he took her into his arms, and he'd have sworn the air sizzled as the *maalem* now sang in English. His raspy voice spoke of how this music spoke to his spirit and his soul; how it spoke of hope for the future, of freedom.

Lily laid her head against his chest and he

felt as though his heart were speaking to her. The scent of her hair was more intoxicating than the glass of wine he'd drunk; the warmth of her body against his, the feel of his hand on her back, all dizzied his head.

Until the music came to an end and they stepped back and stared at each other, still caught in the spell of the lingering notes.

'Darius?' Her voice was soft, but clear and certain. 'I want to seize this moment, enjoy it. Not just this moment, but the next one and the one after that. To experience something I know I want.' Now she gave a small gurgle of laughter. 'To be clear, I want you. Not for ever, not even for long, but definitely for tonight.'

'Then let's go.' Perhaps he should stop, think, but he couldn't. He could see no hint of doubt in her eyes or voice, and knew she spoke simple truth. Not to do this would be unthinkable and so, once they had politely refused dessert and confirmed with the band that they would definitely like them to play at the fundraiser, they were finally able to leave.

Once outside, he couldn't help but laugh, a laugh of happiness as he took her hands in his. She echoed his laughter and then he picked her up and twirled her round, not caring who saw them, realising he had no idea who had taken what photos. This evening had been about Lily—for real.

As he put her down, she placed her hands on his shoulders and brushed the lightest of kisses against his lips. 'Thank you,' she said.

'For what?'

'For being you instead of the person I thought you were.'

The words warmed him.

'Now, let's get back to the villa,' she said. 'Quickly,' she added.

Clasping her hand tightly, he started to run and, half-laughing, breathless, propelled by sheer desire, they made their way back to the villa and went inside and straight up the stairs.

'My room's closer,' she said, and then they were inside. Now it was all about haste, near panic that something would happen to stop this—he didn't think he could bear that. Every sense was heightened, every part of him heated, volatile, ready for her—wanting, needing, to give and receive pleasure.

Stumbling, fumbling, in their haste, finally all their clothes were tangled on the floor and at last he could touch and feel, and then he was kissing her and they tumbled onto the silken sheets of the bed.

* * *

Lily opened her eyes, aware of an immense sense of wellbeing, a lightness, as memories seemed to float on the brilliant white ceiling. The images brought heat to her face as she recalled the glorious kaleidoscope of sensation; the freedom of exploring his body; of learning first hand that it was everything her imagination had believed and more. She remembered the feel of his hands on her, his lips on her, the things they had done, the laughter, the sheer joy...

She shifted and the euphoria faded a tiny bit when she realised the space next to her was empty. Her last memory was of falling asleep, safely cocooned in his arms, in the early hours of the morning.

Don't panic, she told herself.

Perhaps he preferred to sleep alone and had simply gone back to his own room. Maybe that was how short-term, fun relationships worked. Or maybe he'd gone for a shower, or for a walk, or...

The point was it didn't matter—she would not let last night be tainted by doubts. Last night had been about phenomenal, fun sex full of laughter, passion and the type of sensations she had never experienced before. With Tom, it had been pleasant, enjoyable…but nothing like she had experienced last night and this morning. Perhaps with Tom everything had been clouded by her need for love and a happy ending, whereas strings-free sex was different: no doubts, fears or expectations.

So, whatever happened next, she'd be good with it.

Yet when she entered the kitchen half an hour later, showered and dressed in a long floral sundress, she halted on the threshold in the grip of a sudden sense of awkwardness, a shyness verging on embarrassment, when she recalled how abandoned she had been last night. How far she'd been from the professional, cool Lily Culpepper.

'Good morning,' he said and the warmth in his voice and his smile reassured her, though she saw a slight wariness in his eyes, a slight clench to his jaw as he indicated the table by the arched window. 'I'll start breakfast,' he said.

Turning, she saw he'd set the small table by the kitchen window overlooking the mosaic-tiled courtyard where the early morning sunshine pooled, lighting the tiles with flecks of copper and gold. A vase full of flowers was in the middle along with a jug of freshly squeezed orange juice and she smiled. 'That looks lovely.'

'Thank you. I'm making an omelette with chillies and olives, if that's OK.'

'That sounds perfect. Thank you.' The words were slightly stilted as she moved closer to the hob. 'Can I help?'

As she got closer to him, she stopped. 'You used the soap,' she said, inhaling the earthy scent of the black soap.

'So did you,' he said, stepping slightly closer, and she stilled as desire churned, along with a need to bury herself into his neck and inhale his scent...

But neither of them moved closer, though she could see her own desire mirrored in his grey eyes. Instead, he cleared his throat, turned away and picked up an egg. 'You could make coffee, or tea if you prefer it. There's a cafetière, and I got some fresh coffee.'

'Sure.'

Ten minutes later, they were seated. 'This is delicious,' she said. 'Thank you for doing this. You must have got up very early to make it to the shops and back.'

'It's not a problem.'

Silence fell and Lily frowned, part of her not wanting to ask the question, but she knew she had to, her earlier euphoria starting to fade at the edges. 'Is everything all right?' she asked in the end. 'I mean, I feel like there's a problem.'

'No.' There was a pause as he pushed away his plate. 'Yes,' he amended, and now anxiety started to unfurl. Maybe she hadn't measured up… Then he went on. 'I mean, I've never done this before.'

Relief hit her and she couldn't help it—she raised her eyebrows, 'Really? In that case, last night was even better than I thought.'

This pulled a chuckle from him and lightened the tension. 'I'm glad you enjoyed it,' he said. 'So did I.'

'So that's not the problem?' She could hear the hint of a question in her tone and saw the surprise in his eyes.

'No. Emphatically no problem there. I enjoyed every second.'

'So what is the problem?' she asked.

'I've never done what we did last night without having some rules in place, rules that meant I knew how to act the next morning. I was thinking about making breakfast in bed, but I thought that might make you uncomfortable, and I don't like feeling like this—no rules, no boundaries. It's thrown me.'

Lily reached out, placing her hand over his,

and wondered why he needed those rules and boundaries; why he had never once risked a real relationship. 'We didn't need any rules or boundaries to be set. I understood, I understand, that you have no wish for commitment or anything long-term. Last night was…'

She paused, trying to find words as he placed his hand over hers, and the mere touch evoked a frisson of renewed desire, reminding her of exactly how the previous night had been.

'Incredible,' he offered. 'Magical.'

'Both those things, and nothing can or should take away from that.'

But worry still flecked his eyes and her curiosity deepened along with a desire to take that worry away. 'If you're worried about what happened with Ruby repeating, please don't be. I'm completely good with this being one night only. I think your arrangements with Ruby went wrong because Ruby did want a long-term relationship with somebody one day. I don't want a long-term relationship, ever, any more than you do.'

'Why not?' he asked. 'How can you be sure? Not about us, but how can you know you don't ever want that?'

She sensed that the question was asked out of a curiosity that matched her own, perhaps along with a need for validation, a desire to understand why someone else was on the same page as him. To her own surprise, she wanted to share, to explain.

Perhaps because she trusted Darius; after all, they were in this together, both of them protecting their business reputations—a fact that had been emphasised by their meeting with his stakeholders the previous evening. Perhaps because she knew this was a bubble of time and soon enough they would go their separate ways. Maybe because Darius felt like the right person, the man who had blindsided her with an attraction she could never have imagined. A man who made her feel beautiful.

'Because… I don't believe in the traditional happy endings, for me. It's not what I want, because it requires too much trust. Yesterday, when you explained your attitude to relationships, the way you minimise the risk of hurting people and yourself, that made sense. I've seen too many people hurt, seen too often how easy it is to overturn vows of love.'

He reached out and placed his hand over hers. 'Tell me,' he said.

Lily saw the focus in his gaze and knew that here was someone who would truly listen to her in a way no one ever had before. Her mother had rarely had time to listen, or if she had she hadn't got it, and couldn't see life from any other perspective than her own. She was unable to understand or be interested in a daughter who was chalk to her cheese.

Tom… Tom had tried but he had always interrupted, or cut her short, and had never really wanted to hear anything that he deemed as negative. She looked down at their clasped hands, took reassurance from his touch and began.

'My mother is a beautiful woman, a woman with the "it" factor, X factor—every sort of factor. She fell pregnant with me when she was twenty, but I don't know who my father is. All I know is that his parents found out and they bought my mother off. They didn't want her and a baby to ruin my father's life. She took the money, moved away and changed her name.

'Then she decided the best way to live was to target a wealthy married man. She set up an arrangement with him. He bought her a house, paid her bills and he visited often. When I was ten, the liaison came to an end; my mum negotiated a lump sum last payment and moved on. This time, she decided she wanted marriage. She targeted an extremely wealthy businessman. He didn't stand a chance; he divorced his wife of twenty years with whom he had two daughters and married my mum. His wife was heartbroken.'

And his daughters had never forgiven Lily.

'What about you?' he asked. 'Where were you in all of this?'

'I wasn't, really. Mum used to send me off to "friends", and then when I was older it was a mixture of nursery and friends. It wasn't all her fault. She and I…we are so different. She wanted a different type of daughter, a pretty one. I wasn't a very pretty baby or child, really. I guess I got my dad's genes or something. I didn't like being shunted away all the time—especially because her friends didn't really want me—but I preferred it to hiding out in my room and being told to stay quiet.'

She shrugged. 'But, whatever her faults, she provided me with a roof over my head, food and security.' Lily had done her best to appreciate that, even whilst she'd sometimes wished for a more normal mum, the sort who came to sports day, the sort who asked other children round after school.

'She also showed me that fairy tales don't exist. They are illusory, unrealistic; they necessitate placing blind trust in someone with no guarantee they won't break that trust and shatter it into little pieces. Just like so many men did over my mum.'

There was a silence and she saw the intent look in Darius's grey eyes. 'It's more than that, though, isn't it?' he asked gently. 'It's not only your mum who showed you that—you've experienced it yourself.'

Lily stared at him. 'I… How do you know?' she asked.

'Because I know you,' he said. 'I can see how different you are from your mother. You've earned your own way, you've set up a successful business yourself, you're reliant on no one. You haven't followed in her footsteps. I think you would have been the same about fairy tales—you *would* have believed in them.'

Surprise washed over Lily that Darius could have worked this out about her. 'I wanted to believe in them,' she said softly. 'I wanted my mother to be the wicked witch, the wicked stepmother of fairy tales, and I would be the heroine, the princess who got true love and a happy ending. Then I met Tom and he ticked all the boxes. He was handsome, charming and I couldn't quite believe that he seemed to like me.'

She could remember the sense of gratitude she'd felt that someone like Tom would pay her any attention. The idea that she could have it all. 'We started dating and I decided he was "the one". I was determined to be the perfect girlfriend. I cooked his favourite foods, supported his football team, tried to be supportive. Then my mum asked us to dinner, and of course I said yes.' She could hear bitterness in her voice.

'Of course you did; there's nothing wrong with that.'

'But there was, really. I wanted to show him off, show her that fairy tales did exist—that love was possible, that I could win a man.' What she hadn't known was that Cynthia and Gina would be there. She could remember her instinctive recoil when they'd greeted her, and how seeing them had made her appetite disappear at the forced, manufactured politeness. 'My stepsisters were there as well.'

Darius nodded, and his eyes narrowed slightly. She wondered if he could see what was coming. What might be obvious now had seemed inconceivable to her then.

'The dinner was all right, but that's when everything changed. I just refused to see the signs.' She met his gaze. 'That's why I identified with Ruby, because I did exactly what she did—I saw what I wanted to see, rather than reality. Despite Tom cancelling dates at late notice, despite the fact he was different.'

He had called her clingy or needy. He had made excuses not to stay over. But then at other times he had been super-nice, surprising her with dinner and extravagant gifts to make up for being cross, or absent. 'So much so that I decided to propose.'

Her voice caught and remembered humiliation washed over her. 'It was Valentine's Day. I made a romantic dinner. I had a massive helium balloon, a banner that said "be my valentine". It was cringe-worthy, really—every cliché under the sun. I even had violin music playing in the background. Thankfully, before I could actually go down on one knee and ask him, he confessed—told me he'd fallen in love with Cynthia.'

As she told the story, she could taste the bitterness, feel the disbelief. 'Cynthia, who is beautiful—the sort of beauty my mother has, the universal "it" factor, and he'd fallen for it. I tried to tell him she had only targeted him to hurt me.'

She had tried to tell him about the bullying, but he'd refused to listen, the tone of dismissal absolute.

'You can't expect me to believe someone like

Cynthia could do that,' he'd said. 'I understand why you are saying it but you shouldn't try to set me against Cynthia.'

The words, that he believed she would lie about something like that, had been an additional sucker-punch of hurt. And she'd vowed never to tell anyone about the bullying again, to deal with it herself.

'But he just looked at me with such pity in his eyes, and he said it didn't matter, because if he'd really loved me he wouldn't even have looked at Cynthia. And that made me feel…'

'As though somehow it was all your fault?' Darius said and she saw compassion and a genuine understanding in his eyes.

'Yes. That's exactly it. I felt as though I hadn't been good enough.'

'Not true. *Tom* wasn't good enough.'

Lily shook her head. 'It wasn't his fault he fell for Cynthia.'

'No, but not telling you, seeing her behind your back, being unfaithful, leading you on— that was his fault. You say you didn't see the signs, but you shouldn't have had to. He should have told you himself, but he didn't—his bad, not yours. His cowardice was not your fault.'

Lily heard the suppressed anger in his voice. 'And his loss.' He released one of her hands, reached out and tipped her chin so that she was looking straight at him. 'That's why I know that you were, you *are*, better than good enough.'

Lily blinked back sudden tears; it was as though some of the humiliation, the second guessing, was draining away, leaving her lighter. Now she reached out and stroked his cheek. 'Thank you,' she said softly.

A lingering doubt touched her, along with a sense of loyalty. 'And I'm sorry if I sounded negative, especially about my mum. I do know she did her best, gave me security, and I know that I am not the daughter she would have wished for.' She took a deep breath, hoping that Darius didn't think she'd been complaining. 'I just wanted to explain to you why I don't believe in fairy tales. Thank you for listening, and understanding.'

Because Darius did understand; she could see it in his eyes, hear it in what he had said and the way he had said it. She sensed a connection, a solidarity between them, and wondered if he felt the same—wondered if there was a chance he would confide a little in her.

CHAPTER TWELVE

Darius saw the sparkle of tears in her eyes, and wondered if she believed him. He wanted her to; he wanted her to see herself as he saw her—as someone who had succeeded, someone who was beautiful inside and out. He understood her decision to close her heart; how could she trust in love? But he wanted her to believe in herself, to be sure that she wasn't eschewing fairy tales because she didn't believe she was good enough to be the princess, or didn't deserve to be loved. He wanted her to know what a good person she was.

He thought about what Lily had shared with him, full of admiration for how she had handled and processed her childhood. He understood the emotions she must have experienced; for the first eight years of his life, he hadn't known who his father was either, he knew all too well how that could affect a relationship with a mother.

Looking at Lily now, seeing the pain in her eyes, he wanted to help. Strangely enough, even though he knew that meant sharing his own childhood, something he had never done with anyone, that felt all right. Because he knew he could trust Lily, and knew that soon enough their ways would diverge.

'You haven't been negative. I admire how you have kept faith with your mother. How you handled your childhood. You should be proud about that. I wish I could have done the same.'

'Tell me,' she said, echoing his own words of earlier. 'About your childhood.'

'My mum had me when she was in her mid-twenties, and like you it was just her and me. But my mum, though I didn't really understand at the time, was an addict. Alcohol and drugs were her go-to when she was depressed, and that was a lot of the time. Looking back now, I think perhaps she was bipolar, or she'd had a traumatic childhood herself. I don't know.' He could hear the sadness in his voice, the knowledge that perhaps he never would.

'I'm sorry,' Lily said, 'That must have been hard for both of you.'

'It was—she tried her best, but when she was under the influence she couldn't help herself.' There'd been too many times with no food on the table, times when he'd come home to find his mum crashed out on the sofa, the house a tip that he'd cleaned up as best he could.

'But there were good times too—times when she'd tell me stories about pirates and wizards, magical fantasies that I loved. Times when we'd go to the park and eat ice-cream. And there was always a sense that we were in it together. I loved her and I believed she loved me.'

'That is incredibly important in itself,' she said softly. 'I never felt that; I was a duty to my mum, a responsibility she fulfilled, but I never felt we were a team. It always felt as though we were in opposition. It sounds like your mum loved you enough to try to be a good mum.'

'She did and we were managing, but…in the end I messed it up.'

Lily gently squeezed his hand. 'You were a child,' she said.

'But old enough to know better. I was obsessed with the need to know who my father was. I had this fantasy that, if I could find him, he would come and rescue us. Make my mum happy so all the times would be full of ice-cream and stories. That my father would be different from all the other men in her life.' The ones who had scared him, the ones who got drunk, the ones who had made his mum tell him to get lost and disappear, so that he'd crept out for as long as he could.

'You wanted a fairy-tale ending for her,' Lily said. 'For both of you, and you wanted your dad. That's natural. I did too. I fantasised all the time that he'd turn up one day, that he'd track us down. I used to beg my mother to contact him or to tell me who he was. But she wouldn't, and I worked out soon enough that I wouldn't be able to change her mind. So I gave up.'

'I wish I'd done the same. But I didn't. Instead, I questioned her constantly and every time she'd tell me a different story: my dad was a fireman, a footballer, a dustman... Every time she spun me a story, it felt like I had a mission. I'd go and haunt the local football ground, or accountancy offices, look for men who looked like me, even though I knew it made her angry. It was the only thing really that made her angry with me. Maybe she felt I should be happy just with her.'

'Or maybe it made her feel bad about herself,' Lily said, and he stared at her, arrested by the thought. Maybe the anger hadn't been directed so much at him but at herself.

'But you couldn't have known that.' Lily slipped her hand into his, her eyes wide. 'You were a child, trying to help, trying to change your mum's world for the better.'

'Only I got it wrong.' Sadness and self-recrimination, the guilt he had tried to hold at bay for so long, seared him. 'One day, I thought I'd found him—a firefighter, so it tied in with one of my mum's stories. In my head, I looked like him—he'd dark hair and I managed to get close enough to see he had grey eyes.

'I started to hang round the fire station; my plan was to follow him home. Only one day, it was late, he spotted me and he and a female colleague came out to see why I was there. They ended up taking me home to my mum. In my head it was going to be the grand reunion. In real life, it was a fiasco, because my mum was in the midst of a row with a boyfriend. They were both completely wrecked, and there were bottles and syringes dotted around the place. It couldn't have been worse, really. I ended up in emergency foster care. I didn't see my mum again.'

'What?' The word fell from her lips, her eyes wide with shock and consternation.

'She disappeared—cleared out the next day, they said. Left a letter for social services and a letter for me. She said I would be better off without her, and they'd take me anyway, but she'd done her best to give me what I truly wanted—a dad. The letter to social services gave four possible names: Enzo Kingsleigh was one of them. Social services approached him first and it turned out he had had a very brief relationship with my mum. They did a test and it turned out he was my biological dad. He took me in.'

'And the rest is history,' she said softly. 'You were taken in by your dad, given a home and love, security and a whole family…a dynasty.'

'Yes.' He knew his voice sounded colourless, knew too that he wouldn't refute her belief. Because he'd always pretended that had been the case in every interview he'd ever given, hoping by saying the words he'd make them true.

'I'm sorry.' Lily's voice soft. 'I know it's been three years since his death, but you must still miss him very much. But at least you did find him, though I know it came at a bitter cost.'

'I used to wish that I had never followed that firefighter. If I'd known, I wouldn't have done it. Not if I'd know it would drive my mum away.'

Her grip tightened on his hand, giving comfort. 'And that is a tribute to your mum, that you feel like that despite the difficulties. But it wasn't your fault. *You* didn't drive her away.'

She reached out and touched his cheek oh, so gently. 'I know how easy that is to say, but it sounds to me as though something else would have triggered social services to intervene. A teacher may have noticed something, or worse, there could have been an accident. All your actions did was precipitate something that would most likely have happened anyway.'

The words offered balm, as though she understood the guilt he carried, but also as though she believed him. Believed that he would genuinely swap the life of wealth, that he did truly regret what he'd done.

'It just feels wrong that she thought I'd be better off without her; that I had been looking for my dad as a replacement for her. That she thought I wanted her to go—that she didn't try and fight for me.'

'I'm sorry. Did social services try to find her? Did your dad try?'

He shook his head. 'Social services tried, but I have the impression once my dad agreed to take me in they didn't try very hard. As for my dad, he never spoke about my mum; it was as though he wanted to write that part of his life out of Kingsleigh history, out of his own history. I am not sure he even remembered very much of it himself. I think he preferred to believe that my life started aged eight.'

Lily frowned. 'So you were transferred to a completely different world and expected to fit in and forget the past eight years.'

'Pretty much. And to be grateful.' He frowned. 'Sorry, that was unfair. I was grateful. But…'

'You missed your mum.'

'I did.' He could remember now crying into his pillow, wishing, willing, her to come back. 'No one understood that except Gemma. She was in a relationship with my father when I turned up in his life, and she was wonderful; she insisted on being my godmother. But she and my dad split soon after and she disappeared from my life for a while.'

A decision made by Enzo rather than Gemma, though his godmother had re-entered his life as soon as she could. 'But everyone else seemed to think I was well rid of my mum; that she had chosen to leave and that missing her meant I didn't appreciate what I had.'

'She did choose to leave,' Lily said. 'But it sounds as though she knew that she couldn't look after you the way that she wanted to—that she left because she loved you and it was the best thing for you.'

He heard only compassion and sympathy in her voice, no judgment.

'Do you think your mum did what she did because she thought it was the best thing for you?' he asked. 'The best way to maximise security so you could have a good life?'

'She could have got a job,' Lily said. 'To be fair, she believes she did get a job—says she is a businesswoman who made lucrative deals and she has always kept her side of the bargain. She doesn't understand why I don't agree with that.'

Darius picked his words carefully. 'I don't agree with targeting men or breaking up marriages, but maybe there are reasons you don't know about. In the same way I don't know why my mother turned to alcohol and drugs or why she couldn't manage to give them up for me.'

There was a silence and then Lily reached over and put her arms around him. 'Maybe it was just too hard so instead she did something even harder—she gave you up. Maybe over the years she has made a new life for herself. Have you ever thought about tracing her?'

'I decided not to.'

'Why?' she asked.

'Because she knows where to find me. I am in the papers enough; there is no secret about where my headquarters are and there is a myriad of ways she could have got in contact.' He hoped he'd kept the hurt from his voice. 'I have to assume she has her own reasons for not wanting to make contact.'

'I can see that it would be difficult for her. She may think you don't want her to contact you, particularly if she suffers from mental health issues. Plus, she may be worried you would think she wanted money. Or she may see how happy your new life has been and she doesn't want to rock the boat. May still thinks it's best for you if she stays out of your life. It's a lot to think about, but if there is anything you want to say to her maybe you should try to trace her.'

Her words made sense; actually talking about this with someone else made a real difference. Especially as this was a topic close to her heart.

'Have you ever tried to find your father?' he asked.

'No. I thought about it a lot when I was younger but I couldn't work out how. Mum wouldn't even tell me where she was born. Then, when I was older, I decided not to. It didn't seem fair. He might be married with kids. He had no idea I existed and the reverberations would be too great. How would it affect his relationship with his parents? There are too many unknowns.'

'Or you could look at it the other way,' Darius said. 'He may welcome the knowledge. He may have no other children, or he may have children who would welcome you into the family. Especially when they see you have no expectations of them.'

If he'd found Enzo as an adult, when he was a success in his own right, would they have forged a relationship? 'You wouldn't be a responsibility—you're an adult. Maybe you should trace him. Maybe you could persuade your mother to tell you his identity, or persuade her to talk about it more and try to get some clues. Once you know who he is, his circumstances, then decide whether to contact him or not.'

There was an arrested look on her face. 'I've never thought of it like that,' she said. 'When I think about him, I revert to childhood, imagine what it would have been like to find him then. But you're right.' A smile lit her face. 'Thank you. The things you've said, the way you've listened…it's shifted something inside me.' Leaning over, she brushed her lips against his cheek and he caught his breath at her nearness.

Then something shifted; a sense of lightness, of appreciation, came into being and she was in his arms. He kissed her, a kiss that held so much—thanks and appreciation for listening, for understanding for *caring*; a sense of connection from their pasts, a reminder of the night before and a promise of what was to come. Everything intermingled and, when they finally separated, he pulled her to her feet and smiled down at her.

'We missed out on breakfast in bed but I can offer you a different activity…'

'Hmm…what sort of activity did you have in mind?'

'Why don't you come upstairs and I'll show you?' He waggled his eyebrows and she laughed, a glorious infectious laugh, and he laughed too as he tugged her towards the door.

Lily opened her eyes into an instant of confusion and saw Darius lying next to her, his face relaxed in repose. She smiled and stretched gently so as not to wake him, feeling the ache of muscles, and her smile widened as she recalled the extent of the activity of the past hour.

This time passion had been heightened by a sense of languorous exploration, a feeling that now they had more time to tease and tantalise, to scale the heights of need and desire. There'd been a sense of a new deeper connection.

She studied him now, the sunlight from the open window glinting coppery highlights on his dark hair, and she felt something twist inside her at the idea of all he had confided in her, and all she had confided in him. She felt a sense of solidarity at their joint loss: the loss of a mother who had left him, whatever her motivations; a sense of all that might have been if he hadn't gone on a quest to find his father. For her, the loss of a father she'd never known and who would never know that somewhere in the world was a daughter.

Unless she did something about it, as Darius had suggested, the idea taking root and giving her a sense of taking a step in a new direction.

Darius opened his eyes and she was rewarded with an instant sleepy smile. 'I can't remember the last time I had an afternoon nap,' he said.

'Neither can I.' She gave a small gasp. 'But now we'd better get a move on. We are supposed to be meeting Jamal and his team and then I need to go back to the souks.'

He gave a mock-groan and a salute, but she could see that he was smiling goofily, and she had a feeling her own smile was equally goofy.

Because somehow it didn't feel like work—it felt like an opportunity to be with Darius.

Presumably that was how it was supposed to be—a short-term, fun relationship; a safe space in which to share confidences with someone who couldn't hurt her. Now she understood why Darius wouldn't entertain long-term relationships—he knew what it felt like to have someone who loved him, to have someone he loved leave him. So he'd set boundaries in place for protection, to protect himself and the other person. If they knew someone was going to leave, they couldn't abandon you.

He would never open himself up to that again any more than Lily would. She knew trust was too much to ask on a long-term basis and the idea of being supplanted again, being betrayed again, was unacceptable. Both of them understood that and they had both forged alternative happy endings, ones in which they were happy in their own successes.

'Darius?'

'Yes?'

'We haven't talked about…how this is going to work. I know I said this morning I was fine with it being one night, and I was, but now… Well, now we…'

'Landed back in bed without a discussion

again,' he said, sitting up and moving backwards so that his back was resting against the wall. She couldn't help it; her eyes lingered on his chest, the swell and sculpt of muscle.

He grinned. 'And, if you look at me like that, we'll never leave the bed…' Heat touched her face and his grin widened as he reached out, tucked his arm around her and pulled her to his side so they sat pressed together, his strong, muscular thigh pressed against her leg.

'Tell me what you want,' he said.

'I want to have fun, to enjoy this…for a short period of time, before we go back to our normal lives. So…until the end of the fundraiser.' That was five days away. 'Does that work?'

'That definitely works. And I plan to enjoy every single minute.'

'Me too.' Happiness bubbled up in Lily at the idea of five glorious days. Yet as she looked at him, saw the warmth in his gaze as his eyes caressed her body, a sudden doubt assailed her as she thought of the time together coming to an end. She pushed the thought away. Five days: that was long enough to have fun, but short enough not to get attached in any way at all; to be protected by the boundaries, safe in the knowledge there'd be no complications or messy emotions involved.

CHAPTER THIRTEEN

LILY SURFACED RELUCTANTLY from the depths of sleep, opened her eyes and blinked as she saw Darius standing by the side of the bed, fully clothed, in jeans.

'Time to get up,' he said. She looked towards the window, saw that it was still dark and squinted at her watch. 'It's four in the morning,' she said.

'Yup. Surprise!'

She rubbed her eyes. 'You've *got dressed* and woken me up to surprise me? I can think of better ways.'

He grinned. 'Tomorrow morning I'll wake you up at four and surprise you in a different way.'

The banter triggered a jolt of happiness at the knowledge that this was a promise he would keep. 'I'll hold you to that. But seriously, what is going on now?'

'I've got a surprise for you, but you have to get up so I can take you to it.'

The excitement on his face energised her, despite the fact she'd tumbled into bed exhausted. They'd worked really hard: shopped for supplies in the souks, finalised the dinner and canapés menu with Jamal and his team, and met up with the *maalem*. But now she was wide awake, another goofy smile on her face at the idea that Darius had arranged a surprise...for her.

'Give me ten minutes.'

Soon enough she blinked in the early morning air, amazed by the quiet, only now realising how noisy Marrakesh was by day and night. She looked up at the sky tinged with the faintest anticipation of dawn, just as a car pulled up outside. They climbed in the back and Lily focused on watching the landscape go by; the streets deserted now, the shops all shuttered up, the usual fragrance of mint tea absent. Then they left the city boundaries and the road was bumpy now, the only sights a few isolated mosques until the car arrived at a base camp.

'We are going up in a hot-air balloon to see the sunrise,' he said. Moving over to Darius, Lily hugged him, holding the strong contours of his body close, cocooned in his strength.

'Thank you! That is a wonderful surprise.'

They broke apart as a woman approached them, speaking in faultless English as she offered them tea and briefed them on the safety protocols, then gestured towards the adjoining field.

'You can watch the balloon being inflated,' she suggested, and they walked over hand in hand, watching the brilliantly coloured, majestic red-and-yellow balloon billow out and upwards in a whirr of noise.

In a surprisingly short space of time the balloon was pronounced ready, and they walked towards the massive basket and scrambled in. The balloon began its ascent, slowly rising from the ground, swaying in the light breeze, the pilot expertly manoeuvring as they climbed. The ground receded, becoming smaller and smaller as they watched.

Lily felt a soaring sense of freedom as she gazed at the expanse of sky around them, and slipped her hand into Darius's. 'Thank you for this—it is incredible. Up here, I feel as if anything is possible.'

He nodded. 'One thousand feet from the city. It truly does feel we have got away from it all.'

'It does.' Away from the tendril of doubt starting to unfurl about how she would feel at the end of this fling; worries about whether

the fundraiser would be a success and the prospect of the impending wedding—watching
Tom marry Cynthia, everyone's eyes on her,
the knowing looks, the whispers. Up here, that
didn't seem to matter.

'Look…' She pointed ahead at the jagged
stretch of a mountain range.

'It's sunrise,' the pilot said.

They stood transfixed as the rays touched the
looming mountain peaks, stroking and kissing the craggy outlines with hues of yellow,
orange and pink as they crept across, meshing
and streaking the early morning sky, gradually
illuminating the vista.

'I've never seen anything like it!' She turned
to look up at him.

'Neither have I,' he said softly, and she
blushed slightly as he continued to look at her.
What she saw in his eyes sent a glow over her,
because no one had ever looked her like that—
as if she was beautiful—and the idea almost
overwhelmed her. She reached up slightly self-
consciously and tucked a tendril of hair behind
her ear.

'Have I got a mint-tea moustache?' she said
lightly.

'Nope. I just like looking at you. I like the
way your eyes sparkle, and the way your fore-

head creases when you listen.' Oh, so gently he ran a finger over her brow and Lily inhaled sharply as desire shot through her. 'And the sweep of your nose. I like the way your lips turn up when you smile.' Now his thumb rubbed over her lips and she could only gaze up at him. 'I especially like when you look at me like that,' he said.

With that she was in his arms, his lips on hers as the sun rose, burst to its zenith around them and peaked over the mountain tops. She gloried in his kiss, exhilaration and a sweet sense of happiness running through her. Until the pilot cleared his throat and they broke away, half-laughing, to see that a table had been set, laid with pastries, orange juice and tea.

'Please enjoy,' the pilot said, and they went to sit down.

Then breakfast finished, they rose and went to the side of the basket to look out at the view, the sky now a stretch of dazzling cerulean that wisped with soft, fleecy clouds as the balloon took them over clusters of settlements. The brown and red of the earth glowed russet in the early morning sun, and they could see farms dotted over the countryside. Through it all Lily was oh, so aware of the man beside her, and every so often she ran a hand over his arm and felt his fingers at her waist, or he brushed the back of her neck, each touch sending a sear of heat through her.

The minutes drifted past and they floated almost seamlessly through the sky, the imposing velvet silence occasionally intruded on by the burst and flare of the gas burners, a reminder of reality.

Then it was time to descend, and Lily felt a sudden desire to tell the pilot not to do it, to let them stay up here a little longer. But of course she didn't, and all too soon the basket was brought down on a surprisingly smooth landing. They thanked the pilot and clambered out, ready for the journey back to the villa and the day ahead.

And, as if on cue, as they turned for a last glimpse of the balloon both their phones beeped insistently. Lily smiled a rueful smile, looked down and frowned as she saw the message was from Cynthia.

She was truly back to reality with a bump. Bracing herself, she looked down, skimmed the message and frowned again, consternation superseded by anxiety.

'Everything OK?' She heard Darius's voice and quickly pulled a smile on her face.

'Absolutely,' she said. 'What about you?' She

saw his frown, the worry clear in his grey eyes.
'What's wrong?'

He looked down at his phone and grimaced.
'Gemma can't make it to the fundraiser.'

'Is everything all right?' Everything Lily
knew about Gemma indicated that she took
her charitable work seriously. She knew that
one of the perks of the fundraiser would be her
formidable presence, her legendary ability to
generate publicity and persuade the wealthy to
part with their money. She was one of the reasons a lot of people would have bought tickets
in the first place.

'I don't know,' Darius said. 'She says a close
friend needs her.' His jaw tightened. 'She's
asked me to take over as host and to do the
speech.'

She could hear the lack of enthusiasm in his
voice, and wondered at it. He was more than
capable of hosting an event. Then the penny
dropped and she moved towards him, taking
his hands in hers.

'You'll be fine,' she said, suddenly getting
that the speech would be emotive for him—
talking about a charity that helped struggling
mothers so they could have a shot at keeping
their children. Supporting the charity in the
background was one thing, giving his time and

money another, but actually standing up and making a speech would be tough. 'You don't have to make it personal.'

He squeezed her hands. 'Thanks for getting it. I'll be fine. Not as good as Gemma, but I'll do my best.' He nodded at her phone. 'And you're sure you're all right?'

Recalling Cynthia's message, Lily bit her lip then nodded. 'I'm sure.'

Later that day, Darius looked up from his laptop on which he'd jotted the beginnings of his speech. He studied Lily as she stared out of the window at the courtyard beyond, her gaze seemingly focused on the exact same plant she'd been staring at the last time he'd looked up. Anxiety unfurled inside him; she'd been different since they had returned from the balloon ride. She'd seemed distracted, almost withdrawn.

Perhaps she was tired; it had been an early start, after all. Now the anxiety turned into definite jitters. Had he inadvertently done or said something to upset her...or had she changed her mind about the fling?

Chill out.

There was absolutely no point over-thinking this. He cleared his throat, and when that didn't get any response he tried her name. 'Lily?'

She gave a start, then turned towards him. 'Yes?'

'Is everything OK?'

She gave a quick look down, then back up. 'Everything is fine.' She glanced at her watch. 'Do you think we should check in with Jamal and see if he's had any more ideas for the menu or if we need to meet the team again or...?'

'No,' Darius said firmly. 'I don't think we need to do that—Jamal has it all under control.' For a moment, he wondered if Lily quite simply didn't want to be alone with him.

The unwelcome thought put him on edge and he rose to his feet. 'Come on,' he said. 'Let's go for a walk. We can climb the ramparts and watch the sunset... It seems like a good day to do it—sun rise and sunset all in the same day.'

She hesitated and then nodded. 'That does sound good.'

As they started the walk towards the city, he noticed that she was keeping a distance from him; she hadn't slipped her hand into his and he minded, which didn't make sense. He wasn't even a hand-holding guy.

They approached the ramparts. 'We can climb up from here, I think.'

They walked up in silence, both slightly

breathless when they reached the top where they stood, looking over the panoramic vision of the city: the sprawling, chaotic pink-hued buildings; the ochres and earth tones; the bright splashes of colour from the people dressed in robes of yellow, red and blue; the swirling mass of humanity all surrounded by the historic walls and ramparts that enclosed this magical place.

Darius moved closer to her and, when she moved away, his own edginess ratcheted up. 'Something is bothering you,' he said. 'What's wrong?'

At first he thought she wouldn't answer, and then she sighed. 'There's nothing wrong, exactly. I got a message from Cynthia.'

'About Tom?' Scenarios raced round his head. Perhaps Cynthia had split up with Tom. Perhaps Tom had seen what a colossal idiot he had been to give Lily up and now he wanted her back. The thought clenched his hands into fists and he realised Lily was looking at him oddly.

'Sort of,' she said. 'It's from Cynthia and Tom. They've invited you to their wedding, as my plus one.'

'Their wedding?' he asked. 'You didn't mention they were getting married.'

* * *

Lily stared down at the city she had come to love in the past few days, realising he was right. She hadn't mentioned it.

'Partly because I didn't want you to feel sorry for me.' She shrugged. 'But mostly because I didn't want to think about it—like a form of denial.' She hadn't wanted to taint this magical time with a reminder of reality. 'But I'm telling you now. It's a week after the fundraiser, three days before Valentine's Day itself—a Valentine's wedding.'

'Ouch!' Darius winced. 'That's a bit bloody insensitive of them, isn't it?'

'They said they knew I would understand, as it is such a romantic idea. I think they may also see Valentine's Day as the day of Tom's lucky escape.'

'Humph. The boot's on the other foot, if you ask me. I don't even understand why you're going. Unless...you want to show everyone you're fine and you really don't give a damn.'

'That's it exactly.' She wanted to show Cynthia that, if this was another shaft in her 'make Lily pay' arsenal, it had backfired big time. She wanted to show Tom that she'd moved on and made a success of the last two years. 'I won't run away and I won't hide.' She sighed. 'But...'

'You're dreading it?'

'Yes. People will be watching me, feeling sorry for me, and the closer I get to the date the less appealing the whole thing becomes. And now…it's dawned on me that I'll also have to pretend that we're still an item.'

She hurried on, suddenly terrified that she'd sounded sad. 'I know that by the time of the wedding we won't be, but we will still be pretending…' And somehow the thought of pretending, when she'd know the fling was over, twisted her insides with misery.

'I'll come to the wedding.' His words were abrupt, as if he'd surprised himself, and she shook her head emphatically. Damn it, had she sounded needy? Clingy, as Tom had accused her of?

'No. I can't and won't ask you to do that.'

'You didn't ask. I offered.' He shook his head. 'I'm not doing this because I feel sorry for you.'

She looked away, back to the glorious vista below, as the setting rays of the sun wove tendrils of magic onto the imposing upward sweep of the city walls, causing them to glow a crimson hue. Then she met his gaze firmly.

'Then why are you offering?'

'Because I want to be there, with you, by

your side. I don't like the idea of you exposed to pointing fingers and scrutiny.'

There was no denying the sincerity in his voice, and the sense of him having her back, wanting to provide a united front, warmed her, even as the temptation to let him come to the wedding escalated.

'And,' he continued, 'if you want we can extend our fling until after the wedding.'

'Is that what you want?'

'Yes.' There was no doubt in his voice; in fact, his grey eyes lit up with a glow that sent a surge of sheer exhilaration through her, a sense that the sword of Damocles had been lifted. The wedding no longer seemed as if it would be a disaster, and she muffled the voice of caution that pointed out that she was pushing the boundaries, changing the rules set up to protect her, and that that way lay danger.

Nonsense.

They were talking about a few days more, hardly anything; and, damn it, what was wrong with feeling happy about that, about having Darius by her side? What better way to show the world that she'd moved on?

'It's what I want too,' she said. 'Thank you.' Standing on tiptoe, she brushed her lips against his, against the vibrancy of the setting sun, sending shimmers and shades of red and pink across the sky. The kiss was glorious and deep, yet as she pressed her body against his Lily felt it held a bitter-sweetness she didn't understand.

CHAPTER FOURTEEN

TWO DAYS LATER Darius awoke and saw that Lily was already sitting up, her notebook propped on her knees. He shifted up the bed so he was next to her and dropped a kiss on top of her head. She stretched, her leg pressed against his, shoulder to shoulder.

'Today's the day,' he said. The day of the fundraiser.

'Todays the day,' she repeated and sighed, placing a hand on her tummy. 'I have to admit, I'm nervous. I need to tell myself that at least at this time tomorrow, one way or the other, it will be pretty much over.'

He nodded, and relief touched him that it would only be the fundraiser that would be over tomorrow, not their fling, thanks to his offer to attend the wedding. He'd been overcome by a protective instinct that would not let him leave Lily to stand alone against people who had treated her with such sheer, selfish insensitivity. Who were blithely taking for granted her courage and spirit. He would be there to shield her from pointing fingers and, as a bonus, they now had a valid reason to extend their fling.

Lily glanced at her watch. 'The villa guests will be here in a few hours. I need to be ready.'

'*We* need to be ready. We're in this together, remember?' He placed his hand over hers and she shifted closer to him, laying her head on his shoulder, her glossy hair tickling his skin.

'I know; it's just so important we get this right. To recap, we'll greet the guests as a couple, but then for the rest of the afternoon I'll be in my role as housekeeper, making sure they have everything they need. I won't join everyone for dinner, but once we get to the actual dancing and entertainment we will be hosting everything together.'

'The press will be there this evening. Gemma gave exclusive access to one particular magazine, so they'll be interviewing people and taking photos.'

Lily bit her lip. 'We haven't been on show for days, not since meeting Rob and Belinda at the restaurant.'

Could that really have been only four days

ago? 'I don't think anyone will have any problem believing we are together.'

She hesitated. 'I don't think we will have a problem projecting that we are sleeping together but that's not what we want to project. Today I need to be seen as a professional, and so do you. Your stakeholders are attending. We need to get the mix right; need to make this relationship look like more than a fling.'

Lily was right; this was about being professional. 'We'll say we are attending a family wedding together in the next few days, and we'll dial down attraction and dial up…affection. Lovey-dovey isn't professional; little gestures of affection are.' Such as an occasional squeeze of the hand, a light touch on a back, a shared gaze, a quick hug—all things he could recall them doing over the past days when they *hadn't* been on show.

Unease surfaced and he pushed it away as a pointless emotion; even if there was affection, that was hardly an issue. Friends felt affection for each other.

'Gestures it is,' she said as she moved away and climbed out of bed, and he resisted the urge to pull her back. Suddenly he wished there was no fundraiser; that they were here today on a holiday, only answerable to each other. That they could stay in bed all day, entwined in each other's arms, letting desire have its way; that they could read, talk, or venture down to the kitchen to bring picnic meals upstairs.

Darius blinked. Picnic suppers in bed, staying in bed entwined…that was not how fun arrangements went, not today, not ever. And in a few days, after the wedding, this would come to an end and he would be OK with it, because he had to be. The alternative was too messy, too complicated. The unease returned and deepened and he pushed it down. There was no need for disquiet; instead, he should be glad that it would be easy to fake this relationship and that would make their job tonight easier.

Because today was about the fundraiser. He owed Gemma, owed the charity, his full focus on that. He smiled at Lily as she emerged from the bathroom fifteen minutes later,

'We'll be fine,' he said.

Ten packed hours later, Lily acknowledged that so far Darius had been right. Everything had been fine in terms of the fundraiser. The dinner had been a resounding success, Jamal and his team had excelled themselves and she didn't think anyone other than Darius had noticed that

Lily had been one of the waiting staff, standing in for one of Jamal's team, who was ill.

It had given her a chance to observe him at the table and here she'd seen a different man from the one she'd got used to over the past days—a man who cheerfully tackled plumbing problems and wielded a mop. This man fitted in with the super-wealthy. She overheard conversations about things of which she had no knowledge: clubs; fine wines; cars that cost double the cost of her London flat; properties that cost millions; private planes and yachts.

All of it was so out of her ken, but a timely reminder of how far apart their worlds were and that, once this was over, once the wedding was done, she and Darius would go back to their own separate worlds.

The idea was further reinforced by the guests' attitude to her. So far there had been no complaints about the rooms, though Lily had been to and froing with snacks and drinks, providing itineraries, making sure that everyone had everything any super-wealthy person in a luxury villa could possibly need.

And all of them had been suitably appreciative, though she had also seen the curious looks—and sensed some of the politeness at least stemmed from her position as Darius's girlfriend, rather than her position as house-keeper, or even head of Culpepper's.

But now everything was about to change. She was back in their bedroom, changing into her evening dress, ready to greet guests by Darius's side.

'You look beautiful.' Lily gave a small jump at Darius's deep voice, turning from the window as he walked towards her.

'You were looking at my back,' she pointed out.

'Doesn't matter. You always look beautiful to me.' He came to her side, lifted his hand and gently smoothed her brow. 'Don't look so worried. Everything has been amazing so far, and you've got everything covered for this evening.'

His words soothed the anxiety and made him feel less remote, more her Darius. *Whoa. Careful, Lily.* He wasn't hers, and she wasn't his. And he was right: she, they, did have everything covered. That wasn't what caused the nerves fluttering inside her. Those nerves were caused by her worry about facing all these people from his world as his girlfriend.

She glanced down at the simple black dress she'd chosen, designed not to make her too obvious, so that if need be she could slide back into her professional role and float around handing out canapés, or taking coats, and now she was glad of that. She was unsure how she was going to manage discussions about yachts and mansions—unless of course she explained the ins and outs of keeping them clean.

'You're still looking worried.' He smiled at her. 'Maybe this will distract you. I got you a gift.'

'You did?'

'Yup.' He reached into the pocket of his dinner jacket and handed her a rectangle flat box.

She opened the box and her face creased into a smile as her heart did a little loop-the-loop. 'Thank you. I love it.' She took out the charm bracelet, a delicate chain holding four charms: a hot-air balloon, a teapot, a sprig of mint and a gold star.

'To remind you of Morocco and to remind you that you are a star, the best at what you do. And that's why this evening will be a wonderful success.'

A tear threatened as she slipped the bracelet round her wrist. 'Thank you. I'll wear it tonight to bring me luck.' Now she gave him a cheeky smile. 'And I'll thank you properly tomorrow when this is all over. But, before we go down, I've got something for you too.'

She moved over to the bedside table, took

out a small bag and handed it to him, feeling a sudden apprehension. The gift wasn't expensive or designer, or perhaps the sort of gift he would expect. But too late; he'd opened it and she hurried to explain.

'It's a crystal.' They both looked at the yellow-orange stone he held in his hand, smooth and multi-faceted. It glinted in the moonlight, almost as if it exuded motes of magic. 'Called "citrine". This particular one has been cut in a certain way and is of a certain carat and I thought it would fit nicely in your hand. It's supposed to bring luck and positivity and success. I thought it would be a good thing for you to have tonight, when you do your speech.' He hadn't spoken about it, but she knew it was worrying him; she had seen his face as he'd written and rewritten it, tweaked and amended it.

He closed his hand round the crystal, moved forward and pulled her to him in a hug. 'Thank you.' He hesitated. 'No one has ever given me something so thoughtful. I'll treasure it, and keep it in my pocket for later.' He sighed. 'I've made a million speeches and I've never felt nerves like this. I don't even know what I'm nervous about; all I need to do is talk about the charity and the wonderful work it does.'

'For people like your mum, who didn't get help,' she said softly. 'This is personal to you, coming from your heart.' And Darius didn't like emotions; Lily got that, as she didn't either. Feelings, emotions, got you hurt, made life complicated.

'You're right,' he said. 'And thank you again.'

'Ditto.' She gestured to the bracelet.

'So now let's go and do this,' he said, taking her hand as they left the room and headed downstairs, just as the doorbell rang...

And continued to ring as the guests arrived.

Anxiety flashed through Lily with a sense of intimidation reminiscent of years ago: how she'd felt every day at school, every classroom a potential danger; every lunch time, every evening, there'd been someone to face, and she'd been filled with fear and dread at what they had in store. But now, as then, Lily hid her nerves and refused to give in to her fear. She told herself these people were no better than her; that she could face down their curiosity, their disbelief, that Darius was with someone like her. All made easier by the man beside her with his sheer bulk and presence.

And that helped her keep a smile on her face as they greeted guests and mingled. Even when she did feel intimidated by the looks of curiosity, either veiled or direct. Or by the contrast between her attire—the simple black, high-collared, long-sleeved dress, her shoes low-heeled—and the exquisite designer dresses of the guests. Their styles were both elaborate and striking, all worn to catch the eye and be imprinted onto social media and glossy high-society magazines.

But what helped the most was the fact that Darius was clearly so at ease, so happy to introduce her as his co-host, his partner, with his arm round her waist and a private smile, a fleeting touch. He made gestures of affection and, however many times she reminded herself it was a show, damn it, it felt real.

Real enough that she was able to face the press with some level of confidence, even when a reporter asked, 'So, Lily, give me a scoop on you and Darius.'

'Not today,' she said. 'Today I am here in my professional capacity as head of Culpepper's Housekeeping Services. Today is about this fundraiser and the charity it supports. All I want is for the guests to have a wonderful time and for the charity to raise lots of money.'

'And they are having a wonderful time,' Darius said later. 'It's been a complete hit: the stalls round the sides, the storyteller, the music…everything. You did it, Lily.'

She took both his hands in hers, adrenalin and exhilaration running through her, and an emotion she didn't even try to identify as she looked up at him. 'We did it, and now all that is left is your speech. And I know that you are going to rock it.'

She slipped to the back of the seated guests as Darius climbed up onto the stage.

There was no sign of nerves as he stood before everyone, his stance upright, his expression serious. His body, the body she knew so well, was relaxed as he waited for everyone to quieten down, and then he started, delivering Gemma's apologies for her absence and joking about being a less glamorous replacement.

'But whilst I may be less glamorous, considerably so, I feel as passionate and deeply about this cause as my godmother does.' He reached into a pocket and pulled out a sheet of paper.

'This was the speech I intended to give you, and it is a good speech—full of statistics and deserving praise for the charity. But I can summarise this in a few sentences. This charity makes a difference, a true difference, to people's lives—lives that are hard, and difficult. Lives that it is hard for people like us to envisage with our money, the yachts, the holidays, even the ability to attend events like this… If we have an addiction to booze or pills, we can afford expensive rehab facilities. If we have mental health issues, and they are serious, we have access to services, medication, counselling— access to help.

'So it is hard for us to envisage what people without money go through if they suffer from these issues. Only it isn't hard for me…'

Lily clutched the side of her chair, her whole being focused on Darius.

'Someone told me that my support for this charity comes from my heart. She is right. So I want to tell you a story—my story.'

And, up there on that stage, that was what Darius did.

'I have never spoken of my life before I was eight…' he began, and then he explained, leaving out any mention of his dad and simply detailing how hard it had been for his mum to be a good mum whilst battling addiction. 'But, however hard it was, my mum kept trying, trying to do the best she could. In the end, she decided the best she could do for me was to walk away because she had lost the fight with addiction.

'My mother was a troubled, lost soul; a

woman who was prey to the downward spiral of addiction and depression; a woman who tried to pull herself up, but was unable to do so.

'But throughout the eight years I had with her I never once doubted that she loved me, and I loved her. I wish I'd had a chance to tell her that, and most of all I wish she had been able to access the type of help this charity offers to women like her. Women who want to keep their children; who love their children but need some help. So I thank you for all you have done so far—but if you can dig deep and make an extra donation, that would help. It could help women like my mum and the little boy I once was.'

There was a silence at the end, partly stunned, and Lily she could see how moved many people were. Then a woman rose to her feet—a woman Lily recognised as another woman like Lady Gemma, a wealthy woman who tried to use her wealth for good.

'Well said,' she said. 'I wish more people had the courage to speak out as you have, Darius. I'll transfer my ticket money again.'

That set the tone, and Lily smiled to herself as more and more people pledged to do the same. Darius's voice came from the podium. 'I thank you all, as will Lady Gemma when she hears of this. Now I am done, and the band will return and the dancing can begin.'

He climbed down and headed straight towards Lily.

'You were incredible,' she said. 'And so very brave.' And now she didn't care—professional or not, she put her arms around him, stood on tiptoe and brushed her lips against his. She lost herself in the sheer sweetness, wanting him to know how much she admired what he'd done, and they only pulled apart when she became aware of the attention they had drawn. Worry touched her that they'd forgotten the rules, but as she looked round she saw that the guests were smiling at them, almost benignly, probably still caught up in the after effects of Darius's speech. Relieved, she gave him a smile and moved away to help shift the chairs ready for the dancing.

But, as she did so, she overheard two women guests.

'Hmm... Darius and that Culpepper girl—it does look real after all.'

The words made her heart give a little lurch, and for a moment she *wanted* the words to be true—for it to be real.

Then she heard the other woman answer, 'Nah, my dear. That's probably what Ruby All-Star thought.'

Lily almost slammed to a stop, because *they* were the words she needed to hear. She mustn't see things that weren't there, as she had with Tom. This was a fling and a fake relationship—no more, no less. And it was enough. Damn it, it had to be. She would not reopen her heart to a hurt she knew would come. Instead, she'd *enjoy* the next few days...the last few days.

CHAPTER FIFTEEN

THE FOLLOWING AFTERNOON, as they waved away the last of the guests, Darius watched Lily sink down onto a sofa with an exhausted but contented sigh.

'That went pretty well,' she said.

'*Amazingly* well,' he corrected, looking down at her. 'And I get you're exhausted, but there's no rest for the wicked.'

'I know.' She sighed and made to rise to her feet. 'There's still some cleaning up to do.'

'Nope, that's not what I meant. I've re-hired the cleaners to blitz the villa, and you and I are going glamping in the desert.'

Lily shook her head. 'I can't accept that.'

There was something in her tone, something he couldn't quite identify—a withdrawal, a wariness, faintly reminiscent of when they had first met. 'It's not from me,' he explained. 'Gemma arranged it as a thank-you to both of us for taking over from her. Does that make it more acceptable?'

He understood she wouldn't feel comfortable accepting expensive gifts from him; that it would make her feel as if she was following in her mother's footsteps.

'Yes, it does. Thank you for getting that. It is really generous of Gemma; it sounds absolutely incredible.'

When they arrived at the luxury camp, Darius could only agree. White rocky dunes rolled and dipped across an almost lunar expanse that stretched out across a vast, silent landscape. A silence seemed to encompass them in a bubble of timeless tranquillity. A handful of domed yurts were dotted around at more than enough distance to ensure complete privacy.

'Wow...' Lily breathed when they entered theirs. The inside was the epitome of minimalist yet comfortable chic: a massive bed; cool, cream walls; rattan lamps; a splash of colour from the Berber rugs. There was a bathroom complete with shower, and a private patio outside hosted a hot tub. The whole thing brought the sense of an oasis.

Darius glanced down at his phone. 'And dinner is being brought to us here.'

The meal lived up to the accommodation, the tagine spicy and aromatic, the couscous fluffy and tasty, all of it made even better by Lily's presence. Now the fundraiser was over, now they were no longer colleagues, something felt different as they laughed and talked, completely relaxed in each other's company.

The feeling was novel, and he suddenly wished it didn't have to end—that they could live in this yurt for ever. Instead, he would try to make this night count, because after tonight he wouldn't see Lily until the wedding. And after that... He closed the thought down.

'How about we hit the hot tub?' he suggested. 'We can sit in the starlight.'

Ten minutes later, he'd located champagne and they sat in the bubbling swirl of heated water, looking up at the star-swept sky, each pinpoint of light stark against the darkness. The whole vista utterly awe inspiring.

'It's majestic,' she said. 'It literally takes my breath away.' Just like she did to his, he thought as she turned to smile at him with the smile he'd grown to appreciate, the one that lit her eyes, her face illuminated by it. 'Gemma couldn't have picked a better place,' she said. 'But she didn't have to do this. I enjoyed every minute of this job.'

'She wanted to do it. She knows how much you did.'

'How much *we* did,' she said. 'Your speech… I meant what I said last night—it was brave, it was true and it did come from your heart. And I hope it makes your mum come forward.' She hesitated. 'It was good of you not to dwell on your dad. You acknowledged she wanted you to have a better life but you didn't detail your relationship with him—how he gave you more than wealth. How he gave you love, family, a dynasty, a chance to pursue your dreams…'

In that moment, Darius knew he couldn't let Lily keep believing the myth. For what? For whom? He trusted Lily not to betray his confidence, and here and now he didn't want to live the lie any more. Here under the stars, with the vast expanse of the desert stretching out, scorched by the rays of the sun by day and churned by camels' hooves throughout the ages. Here and now he wanted Lily to know the truth.

'It wasn't like that,' he said.

Lily turned to face him, the flicker of light from the soft fairy lights dancing on her face and highlighting the gloss of her brown hair, dancing little motes over her cheekbones and lighting up the dark-blue eyes.

'My dad didn't want to be a father. I think

he hoped when he took me in that that would change, but it didn't. He just couldn't love me. Maybe it was my fault. Maybe I tried too hard—was too needy, too clingy. But mostly he seemed to see me as someone who could have, should have, been someone else's child. I was a reminder of a time in his life when he was "in the gutter, slumming it".'

'Did he say that?' There was outrage in her voice.

'Not to me, but in my hearing. I was a quiet child. I tried to not get in the way, and it meant sometimes everyone forgot I was there and I heard things not meant for my ears. To my dad, I was never a real Kingsleigh, even though I spent every waking minute trying to prove that I was—to him.'

'And to yourself?' The question was gentle.

'Yes. I wanted to belong.'

'You were a child—of course you craved acceptance and love. I did too.'

'But you wanted acceptance on your terms,' Darius said.

'Yes, I did. But I hadn't just been catapulted into a new world where I was suddenly reliant on a new parent, one who I had craved to find all my life.' She paused. 'I assumed that once your dad found you he'd loved you and it was a fairy-tale ending, because that's what I always assumed, dreamed of, as a child. That my dad would turn up and treat me like a princess, would love me for being me. It was natural for you do anything to win your dad's acceptance and love. A love that should have been yours unconditionally.'

The knowledge that Lily truly got it comforted him, as did her sheer presence next to him in the gently bubbling water.

'I tried so hard. I looked up old photos of my father, tried to do my hair like him. When I got older, I dated, I partied and I made headlines. I went to work in the hotel, even though he didn't seem that keen. My cousins all went into management jobs from the get-go. I was told I had to "prove" myself…work my way up from the bottom. I didn't mind—that made more sense to me.'

'But it still hurts, to be treated differently. Did you get on with your cousins?'

'Not really—it wasn't all their fault. They could see how my father felt about me, and they followed suit. Said my blood was "tainted".'

Now her anger was palpable, reminded him of the time she had stood up to the men bullying Aline. 'That is horrible, unfair and cruel.'

'But they believed it and I suppose I did too.

Because in the end, no matter what I did, my dad never loved me, never accepted me, never believed in me.'

'He must have been proud of your business, and the way you set it up.'

'No, he wasn't. I went to him with the idea. I thought that would prove beyond all doubt that I was a true Kingsleigh. He wouldn't give it the time of day. Said I didn't have what it took to get it off the ground anyway.'

The words had hurt and had cut him to the very quick 'So I went back to working for the Kingsleigh empire because I still hoped that that would show him I was worthy.' He shook his head. 'Ridiculous; I should have had the guts to stand up for my idea and gone and done it whilst he was still alive.'

'But you needed his backing.'

'No, I didn't. He would never have given me that. In fact, he made sure I would never have it.'

'I don't understand.'

'He left me nothing in his will. Not a penny, not a single share.' He shrugged. 'The money doesn't matter—he owed me nothing. The shares hurt, though, because it shows he truly saw me as tainted, not a true Kingsleigh. What hurt most was what he said in the will: "for my natural son, Darius, I leave my best wishes and my admiration for how hard he tried". I wish he could at least have left me his love.'

There was a long silence as the words rebounded into the vastness of the desert, the reality stretching across the miles of sand, dispersing up to the stars. The reality that Enzo Kingsleigh had not loved, respected or even liked his son had always made him believe he was unworthy of the Kingsleigh name.

'I'm sorry,' Lily said softly. 'I wish he had, but the fact that your father couldn't give you love is a reflection on him, not you. You're a good person, Darius. You tried so hard—you didn't give up trying, and there is nothing wrong with that.'

'Isn't there?' he asked. 'To try so hard and fail? That's the legacy he left me—that I tried to be a Kingsleigh, tried to win his love, and I failed on both counts.'

'No. He failed, not you. I promise you that.'

He smiled at her. 'Thank you,' he said. 'For listening, for saying the words you've said.' Though he wasn't sure he believed them.

Now Lily turned to him, her blue eyes serious and her hands clenched into small fists. 'I mean it. It's not you who is tainted, it was him. He was not worthy to have a son like you.

He didn't deserve the gift he was given—the chance to be a father to someone so loyal, kind and so incredibly worthy. And I do hope he is looking down now, looking down and seeing what a success you have made without his tainted money. How you have achieved your dream. And that is something to be incredibly proud of. But you can be proud of so much more—your kindness, your compassion, being the man you are...'

Darius heard sincerity in her voice and it seemed to thaw something inside him. Lily cared on his behalf. Shifting now, he pulled her into his arms, looked into eyes that glistened with tears for him.

'Eyes like starlight,' he said softly. 'Don't cry. It's OK. In the end, I achieved my dream my way. His opinion was never going to change, and I have to accept that.'

'But that's not always easy, is it—forgiveness or acceptance? I have accepted that my mum doesn't understand me, that I'm not the daughter she wanted, but it isn't easy. I still want her acceptance—her love, even. But a parent's love should be unconditional, not based on looks or whether you are like your ancestors. If I had a child, I'd love that child unconditionally and I'd want to support them in following their dream, regardless of whether it was my dream. And I'm betting so would you.'

An image came into his head: a little boy walking in the park, scrunching leaves, eating ice-cream, hand in hand in the middle of Darius and a woman with glossy brown hair and dark-blue eyes, the three of them laughing and talking, feeding the ducks... He blinked hard, chasing the images away. That was not possible, and he knew that—not for him.

'I can't take that bet,' he said. 'I'm not planning on being a dad. Short-term relationships don't really allow it.' The words were a reminder to himself and he saw something flit across her eyes.

'For the record, I think you would make a great dad. If not via a relationship, then maybe you could adopt.'

'You'd make a great mum,' he said softly. 'However you choose to do it.'

She gestured towards the sky. 'Look up at all those stars. I wonder, if we could read them, if they would tell us what the future holds for each of us.'

But he didn't want to think about the future. Instead, he traced the outline of her face and held it gently in his hands. As she moved forward to kiss him, something shifted inside him. This kiss held so much warmth, compassion, understanding and a weight of desire that seemed to transcend even the pleasure of their previous nights. Every touch, every sensation, was heightened, intense, beautiful and glorious as they entwined under the stars.

CHAPTER SIXTEEN

THREE DAYS LATER, Lily stared out of the window at the wintry London sunshine and gave a little shiver, despite the fact the hotel room was more than adequately heated. How far away Morocco seemed now. She and Darius had left the day after their night beneath the stars. She'd flown to London and he'd flown to LA—to their different worlds. And every day she'd woken up missing the vibrant Moroccan city with an intensity that surprised her.

Or perhaps it wasn't Morocco she missed but Darius. The thought was unwelcome; missing him had not been part of the deal. But ever since they'd fallen asleep under the stars, wrapped in each other's arms, she'd been aware of a kernel of dread inside her, a sense of impending pain that had deepened with each day apart. Each day had inexorably ticked on towards the day of the wedding—their last day, their last night, together.

And now it was here, the wedding day, and Darius was on his way from the airport.

There was a knock at the door; she went to open it and blinked in surprise.

'Gemma?'

Gemma Fairley-Godfrey stood there, a smile on her face.

'Lily. I hope you don't mind me turning up unannounced.'

'That's fine, please come in. How are you? Is everything all right?'

'Yes, it is. I wanted to thank you in person for everything you did for the fundraiser. I am sorry I couldn't be there. A dear friend of mine was very ill and he took a turn for the worse. Luckily, he is now on the mend, but it was touch and go and I couldn't leave him.'

'I am glad he is better. And thank you for the wonderful gift you gave us.'

'You deserved it. But there is another reason I am here. I have a favour to ask you, and Darius told me where I could find you. Would you mind wearing this to the wedding?' She placed a large bag on the bed and pulled it open. 'It's by a protégée of mine, an up-and-coming designer. I think you would be the perfect person to show it off.'

'Me?' Lily felt slightly bewildered. 'I'd love to help but it may not fit, or…'

'It will. I asked Darius for his help with measurements.'

'So this is Darius's idea?' Lily wasn't sure how she felt about that.

'Nope, it was my idea, and I asked him for some guidance.'

She looked at the dress she had been going to wear, lying next to the brilliant blue concoction Gemma had brought. Her grey offering looked drab, designed to make her invisible, which was exactly what she wanted to be at this wedding.

'The problem is, I'm trying to fly under the radar at this wedding.'

Lady Fairley-Godfrey gave a most unladylike snort. 'With Darius at your side? Not going to happen. Trust me, Lily, you will not be under the radar—and, if people are going to be looking at you, give 'em something to look at. That's what I've always said. Now, I must be going. Thank you again.'

With that, she was gone.

Lily stared at the dress and thought of Gemma's words, knowing that she was absolutely right. No way would she be able to escape attention, not only because of Darius, but because a good number of the guests would know she was Tom's ex and had been jilted in favour of the bride.

So she had a choice: creep around like a little mouse, trying to be invisible, or give people something to look at. Why not look good, for the world to see? And for Darius to see; after all, this was their last night, so she should make it one to remember. This was an opportunity to imprint herself on his memory banks and she wanted that.

Before she could change her mind, she pulled on the blue dress. It could have been made for her. The blue brought out the colour of her eyes and she could hear Darius's voice saying, 'eyes like starlight'. Silvery stars shimmered over the material that flared and swirled, skimming over her figure in silken folds. It was perfect—not so ostentatious that it would take attention from the bride, but enough to make her visible.

There was another knock at the door, another surprise at seeing her mother.

Maria stood in the doorway, mouth agape. And then she said, 'Thank God. You've come to your senses at last and decided to make an effort. Sit down and let me do your make-up.'

Lily opened her mouth to refuse and then suddenly recalled Darius's suggestion that perhaps her mother had reasons for her actions—reasons Lily didn't know about. She could see wariness in Maria's eyes, an expression that expected, was braced for, rejection. Yet her mother kept trying. Just like Lily did. Neither of them walking away from the other. Maybe Maria did want to connect with her daughter and this was the only way she knew how. So Lily nodded. 'OK, I'd like that. But please, nothing over the top.'

Surprise and pleasure touched her mother's perfectly made-up face, though her voice was tart. 'I know what I'm doing.'

Fifteen minutes later, Lily looked at herself and had to admit that her mother did indeed know what she was doing. The make-up was perfect, subtle but effective, making her dark-blue eyes seem larger, her lips glossy and alluring.

'There,' Maria said. 'You'll knock them all dead and no one will think you are pining away. Thank God you aren't wearing that grey dress. If people are going to be pointing fingers at you, then give them something to point at.'

Lily blinked at being given the same advice twice in five minutes by two different people. 'Thank you, Mum. And, Mum?'

'Yes?' Maria turned at the door.

'You look stunning. No one will believe you are the bride's stepmother.'

'Thank you.' Maria gave her daughter a startled look and a sudden smile before she left, and a few minutes later there was another knock. This time Darius came in, and an absurd shyness touched her as he stood stock-still and looked at her.

'You look beautiful,' he said, and her heart sung at the look of sheer appreciation in his grey eyes as they roamed over her body. And there and then she decided, the hell with it—tonight would be the one time when she'd allow herself to believe she was beautiful. A night when she'd seize the moment, let the magical dress cast a spell and allow her to revel in this moment, knowing it would be their last one together. There would be no more thoughts of sadness, just anticipation and happiness that he would be by her side.

'You're looking pretty good yourself.' In jeans and a heavy cable-knit jumper.

'I don't suppose we have time to take the dress off?' he asked.

'No.' Her voice was regretful. 'You need to change, and we need to go, but there's always later.'

'How are you doing?' he asked, and at first

she wasn't sure what he meant. Then she was startled to realise that she hadn't given Tom or Cynthia a thought.

'I'm fine,' she said. 'I feel like I should be angry, or sad, but I'm not.' She'd been more caught up in thoughts of Darius than thoughts of Tom and Cynthia.

Even later in the church, as she watched Cynthia walk towards Tom, Lily felt nothing—or at least, nothing negative. She was able to watch the ceremony with equanimity, and to her surprise she could see the love on both their faces. She realised that Tom had never looked at her that way and, if she was honest, neither had she looked at him the way Cynthia did.

As they exchanged their vows all she was aware of was Darius, his strong body next to hers, his hand tightly round hers. As she looked up at him, he smiled down at her. Then it was over and they followed the bride and groom out into the fresh, crisp February afternoon, watching as confetti was thrown.

Lily studied the faces of the guests, recognised the girls from school and instinctively moved closer to Darius. She was surprised herself at the intensity of her reactions as memories threatened to surface. She told herself not to let it spoil her day, spoil the magic, ruin their last hours together.

'You OK?' Darius's voice was deep, his grey eyes searching as he looked down at her.

'Yes. But I'd like to stick close to you, if possible. I don't really want to engage in more conversation than I have to.'

'Then feel free to stick as close as you like. I won't leave your side.'

True to his word, he didn't, stayed next to her through the sit-down dinner and the speeches. Somehow with him by her side her ex-schoolmates lost their terror, and by the time the band came on Lily was filled with a sense of euphoria.

As they danced, with his hands clasping her waist, her head against his chest, the hard length of his body against hers, she allowed herself to live entirely in the moment. Lost herself in the strains of the music, in the feel of him, the scent of him and the sheer safety of him—the man who had made this day bearable.

More than bearable—almost magical.

The song finished and she stepped back. 'I need the loo, so I'll unstick myself from you for a few minutes.'

She walked away from the dance floor and

saw that her mother was waiting for her, her face concerned.

'Is everything OK?'

'I don't think you're playing your cards right,' Maria said flatly. 'You're all over him. He's with you for the novelty factor, for that feeling that for once he's not being chased or cornered. If you want this to last for a while, you have to play the game, Lily. I know you don't want to hear this but a man like that… you have to work to keep. Look around you— look at the women here who are eying him up. That's part of life. Don't be foolish enough to trust Darius.'

The words made the magic start to dissipate around the edges, because it didn't matter. In a few hours, in the grey light of the morning, this would be over, all the cards played.

'Play hard to get and make sure you work out what you want from your time with him. Whatever it is—money, fun, publicity—it's a bargain. Remember that.'

Her mother of all people had hit the nail on the head. It was a bargain, one she'd entered into blithely, sure there'd be no possibility of being hurt. She watched Darius now, standing on the edge of the dance floor, Gina walking towards him. Gina, the stepsister who had hated her most, even more than Cynthia had.

Lily felt a sudden cold hand clutch her chest. There was no denying her older stepsister's beauty; it outclassed even Cynthia's. Glossy blonde hair fell in a freefall of gold to frame a face of delicate features: cornflower-blue eyes fringed with long, dark lashes; a pert, straight nose. Her figure was that of a super-model. And Lily had a sudden urge to run towards Darius, arms outstretched, stand in front of him and say, 'Mine!'

Only, he wasn't hers.

Was that why she'd wanted to stick close? Had it been some sort of possessiveness, a desire to prevent him from straying? Panic-stricken hurt churned inside her as Gina reached Darius and whispered something in her ear.

She had to calm down. Darius was not Tom. He would not flirt with anyone when he was here with Lily. But he was only with Lily for another night. This was temporary. Sure, they were going to fake a long-distance relationship for a while, but soon enough Darius would be a completely free agent. The idea of Darius with someone else sent a sear of pain straight through her, and she forced herself to turn and walk away towards the bathroom and closed herself into a cubicle.

She sat for a while, then she rose, about to exit, when she heard a group of women enter, recognised their voices and suddenly felt as if she were back at school. The people who'd made her childhood miserable were all grown up now, but it felt as though the years had not passed, and she shrank back against the wall.

'Well, I never thought I'd see this.'

'I feel sorry for her. A man like Darius Kingsleigh will never stay with her.'

'Maybe she told him about how Tom left her for Cynthia, so he's being kind.'

'He'll be quick enough to dance with Gina, given the chance, I'll bet.'

'Poor Lily. Maybe we should tell her not to be so obvious—did you see the way she looks at him?'

Lily stood frozen. How did she look at Darius? How did she feel about him? She became aware of the sudden silence from outside and knew they had noticed the closed cubicle door. She reminded herself she wasn't that frightened school girl any more, pulled in a breath and pushed open the door.

'No need to worry. I heard you all loud and clear. Thanks for the advice.'

With that, she walked out, proud at least that all their faces registered surprise at her words. They'd probably known all along that she was in there, but they didn't matter, not compared to the thoughts and emotions swirling round her brain and causing her tummy to churn in panic. How *had* she been looking at Darius?

She stepped forward and saw him still standing on the edge of the dance floor, still talking to Gina. Emotions shot through her: jealousy, panic, irrational, overriding hurt and a deep sense of possessiveness. This was an overreaction; he wasn't doing anything.

For now.

But what about the future?

She had no hold on Darius and, whilst he wouldn't be crass enough to date Gina, he would inevitably date *someone* else.

How had she looked at Darius? Like a woman in love. Her steps faltered at the sheer enormity of the realisation, as if she'd had a glass of champagne too many, even though she hadn't. She hadn't needed champagne because she'd been giddy on love, even if she hadn't known it. She'd fallen for him, for Darius Kingsleigh—just like Ruby AllStar had.

Lily closed her eyes and opened them again. She would not make a fool of herself at this wedding. She would not make a fool of herself at all. Not again, not like she had two years ago. Unlike Tom, Darius had done nothing wrong. She'd known the terms; hell, she'd instigated them herself. Now she'd see them through and would retain some dignity and self-respect. She would see out this night without letting him know what she'd so foolishly done, for her own pride and for him. He had never wanted to hurt her, and she couldn't, wouldn't, see self-recrimination in his grey eyes, nor pity.

She knew there was no hope that he would return her feelings, but even if he did, or believed he did, Lily didn't believe in for ever. Inevitably, Darius would hurt her. Their time together would be all about waiting—waiting for when the next beautiful woman came along, always looking, always circling. And she knew, of course she knew, that at some point she would lose. Her novelty factor would wear off.

Straightening up, she headed towards him where he now stood alone. She saw his face light up as she approached, and wanted to run towards him, but she didn't. Instead she forced herself to try to look like the same woman who had left the dance floor such a short time before.

'Welcome back. I missed you.' The words

should have warmed her heart, but somehow made her want to cry. 'I was thinking,' he continued. 'Can we talk?' Before she could answer, the music came to a stop, a grandfather clock started to strike midnight and Lily found herself counting the chimes.

As the final bong tolled out, Cynthia entered the room, now changed into her going away outfit, to shouts of, 'Hurrah!' from the guests. Her stepsister headed straight towards her and Lily braced herself. But, to her surprise, Cynthia enveloped her in a hug, a hug that felt real. 'I want you to know I'm sorry—but I do love him. I promise.'

Cynthia stepped back, leaving Lily to process the words, words that seemed to mock her, though she truly didn't grudge Cynthia her happiness.

'I'm glad,' she managed. 'Truly, I am.' And she was. Her time with Tom now seemed muted and a long time ago, as though it all happened to a different Lily.

Then the bride and groom were gone in a swirl of well wishes and blown kisses and the guests began to disperse, heading to the bar for a final drink or to their rooms, and Lily turned to Darius, remembering his question.

'Of course we can talk. Maybe we could

find a room down here somewhere?' She knew she wasn't ready yet to go back to their bedroom, needed some space, some time, to process her fevered thoughts and work out how to get through this last night, this precious last night, without betraying herself. A conversation would help that. She could only assume he wanted to discuss the plan for fizzling out their relationship.

'But first I'll go up and change.' She knew she had to get out of this dress, a dress that had used up all its magic and now symbolised nothing but the illusory promises that fairy tales made.

Turning, she headed for the exit.

Darius watched her go, a small frown on his face as he went and secured a small private lounge for them to talk. Something had shifted in the past half hour but he wasn't sure what. Perhaps it was the finality of seeing Tom marry Cynthia. It would be natural for old wounds to have reopened.

The idea caused a sharp sear of something akin to jealousy. For him, today had been magical. He'd wanted to be by Lily's side as she had requested, had been touched at the request; he'd wanted to protect her from gossip or vulgar curiosity. Wanted to show the world that Lily was a desired, beautiful woman who he appreciated. That Tom had been a fool to give her up.

Though, if Tom was a fool, then what did that make Darius? Because he too was giving Lily up after today, when there was no need. They were planning to continue the fake relationship long distance for a while, use social media and the occasional meet up to keep the ruse going, then let it all fizzle out. In which case why not carry on the fling for real? It would mean changing the boundaries, changing the rules, but they'd already done that once and there was no reason not to do it again.

As if on cue, Lily entered the room, dressed now in jeans and an oversized sweatshirt, her hair pulled back in a ponytail and face scrubbed of all make-up. To him, she looked just as beautiful now as she had in the glittering dress. 'Hey,' he said, as she came in.

'Hey.' She sat down opposite him and he poured her tea.

'What would you like to talk about?' she asked, her voice polite but wary. She was a far cry from the vital woman in the blue dress who had danced with him, laughed with him, held his hand and looked at him with sparkling eyes and a beautiful smile. Anxiety began to unfurl inside him, and he stamped down on. It had been an emotional day; she must be exhausted.

He took a sip of tea and told himself to get on with it. 'I was thinking and… I think that we should extend our fling, keep seeing each other for longer.'

His hands clenched round the arm of his chair, his heart beating faster as she met his gaze. Her blue eyes were wide with shock, but also with something he would swear was sadness.

'Why?' she asked, the syllable stark.

'Because it makes sense. We are going to continue a fake relationship—why not keep having fun? We enjoy each other's company, and we like each other, so really, why not?'

Her gaze dropped to her hands, twisted together on her lap, and now his anxiety morphed further into a sense of dread, a doomed knowledge of impending rejection.

'Because it wouldn't work. It's not what we agreed, and…' She hauled in an audible breath. 'It's not what I want.' Her gaze met his. 'It's too risky. If we make this real, there's too much risk of hurt. It's not personal,' she said. 'It's true of any relationship. We both agreed that and we both agreed to end this here, tonight.'

The words hit him with a stark force, a sucker-punch of pain that shouldn't be possible. His hands gripped around the arms of the chair as he forced his voice to remain calm, as he tried to process why this hurt so much. Every word she said made sense: stick to the rules and boundaries he'd set.

Had there been even the slightest hint of a question in her voice…? He studied her face, but there was nothing. Her expressive face, that he'd thought he could read with such ease, was shut down. She meant it: it was over. He'd never hold her again; they'd never walk hand in hand, never sit in companionable silence or discuss their hopes and dreams. It was over.

'I appreciate everything,' she said. 'It's been fun and…magical. A wonderful moment in time. But now it's time to move on.'

He'd been so sure she would want to take this further. But he'd got it wrong. Lily had been upfront about what she wanted: a short term, no-strings arrangement. She wanted magic and wonder for a few days.

If he'd thought the lines had blurred, that was his own fault.

She held out her hand, then dropped it. 'And I hope all your dreams do come true.' With that, she turned and left the room, and all Darius wanted to do was get up and go after her, persuade her to change her mind, persuade her to…

To what—to continue something she had decided she wanted to end? What would that achieve? What was the point? What did he have to offer? He had believed Lily was worth risking changing the rules for, but she didn't feel the same way about him. He wasn't really surprised. That was how these things worked— they were fun and magical for a short time. But moving on wasn't supposed to be so devastating.

He sat there staring into the fireplace, into the early hours of the morning with the bleak knowledge that it was over; that again someone had found him not worthy.

CHAPTER SEVENTEEN

LILY STARED OUT of the window and tried to take heart from the weak glow of sunshine in the cloudless sky. She tried to see it as a sign that things were getting better, because surely by now the jagged tear in her heart should be healing a little bit?

She'd thought she'd known devastation when Tom had broken up with her but, looking back now to those days when she'd turned to tubs of ice-cream as solace, she could see that it hadn't been her heart that had been broken, but her pride. It had been the humiliation of it; it had been the fact that it was Cynthia who had captured Tom that had devastated her.

This feeling now went so much deeper than that. She missed Darius so much that her muscles felt clenched in constant misery. How she wished comfort could be found in a tub of ice-cream, but she knew it couldn't. Her appetite was gone, though she forced herself to eat, knew she needed the energy to keep working.

She could derive a faint glow of pride, of satisfaction, from the number of jobs that had come in thanks to Lady Gemma Fairley-Godfrey's endorsement, approval and personal recommendations. And of course Lily was pleased. At least it gave her something to do, a distraction from the gaping emptiness that hollowed inside her.

She felt a sense of regret... Why hadn't she extended their fling? Why hadn't she taken him up on the offer? Sometimes the urge to call him, say she'd changed her mind, nearly overwhelmed her. But she hadn't done it. Because, if it hurt this much now, how much more would it hurt in the future?

She forced her mind back to the proposal she was trying to put together, looking up as there was a tentative knock on the door. 'Come in.'

The door pushed inward to reveal her mother.

'Mum?' Lily rose to her feet. Maria had never visited her office. Lily was surprised she'd even been able to find it. 'Is everything OK?'

'That's what I came to ask you.' Maria glanced round the office. 'You've done a nice job here,' she said. 'Just the right amount of understated elegance to show class rather than ostentation.'

'Thank you. That's exactly what I was aiming for.'

'But I haven't come here to discuss décor. You've been ignoring my messages.'

'I've been busy. Catching up after being away. And there's been a lot of new business.'

'That's great, but that's also not why I'm here. I'm here to talk about you, and Darius. And to apologise.'

Lily had never heard her mother apologise to anyone, let alone her.

Maria took a deep breath, and another. She looked uncomfortable. 'I got it wrong. I wanted you to make the same decisions I made in my life and that's not right. I've seen how devastated you are. I can see the misery on your face, in your heart, and I know what that feels like. I never wanted to go through it again and I never wanted you to go through it at all.'

Surprise vied with shock at her mother's words. 'Tell me,' Lily said.

'Your father…' And now Maria had a dreamy look on her exquisite face as she looked back on a past she had never mentioned before. 'I loved him. I know I was young, and idealistic, but I loved him. I always knew it was doomed.

Our families came from different worlds—my dad was in and out of prison, my mum drank, and your dad, he was upper-middle class, with a political family. But we fell in love.

'It was a magical year. We both kept it from our respective families, made plans about a future. He wanted a career in politics, really thought he could make a difference, and I vowed I'd support him. Then I fell pregnant and...'

Maria's voice broke. 'I went to tell him—went to his house because I didn't know what else to do. Told the housekeeper who opened the door that I was a friend. But, instead of him, his mum came to meet me. Somehow she guessed I was pregnant. I was so overwhelmed by their house—by how she looked, how she sounded—and she persuaded me. She made me believe that if I loved him the best thing I could do was leave him. That marrying into a family like mine, having a baby now, would ruin his life and his chance of achieving his political dreams. She told me about his life, the sort of girls he was used to. She offered me a massive amount of money if I would go away and not tell him about you. And I agreed.'

Lily could see the tears in her mum's eyes, knew her own tears were imminent and reached out and took her mum's hand.

'I took the money and I left—left the house, left the city, left my family. But, please believe me, I did it because I loved him, not for the money. I needed the money for you. I had no qualifications, nothing. It turns out I am dyslexic. Back then I thought I was stupid, that I'd couldn't have a career, so yes, I took the money. But I missed him so much and it was hard, being pregnant on my own in a strange place, then being a mum.

'And when I met Max… I knew he was married, but I couldn't bring myself to care. He was kind and he was…someone. The money was running out and…'

'I understand.' And Lily did. She could picture how weary, how sad, how disillusioned her mother must have been. 'And, if Max brought you happiness and security, then I am happy for you.'

'Thank you.' She looked Lily straight in the face. 'I don't regret my time with him or after we split my marriage to Richard. Richard wasn't happy in his marriage, and if it hadn't been me it would have been someone else. And we have been—we are—happy. I have grown to love him—not the way I loved your father, but it is a real love for all that. What I do regret is my relationship with you. I know I haven't always been a good mum.'

Lily raised her hand. 'Don't, Mum. It's OK.'

'It's not, but you and I have plenty of time to sort things out.'

'I'd like that.'

'But first please listen to my advice. If you love Darius, you should tell him the truth. Don't walk away like I did, without giving him a chance. Without giving love a chance. It's a risk, but…it's a risk worth taking. I wish I had.'

Maria glanced at her watch and then rose to her feet. 'Now, darling, I have to run. I've got a facial booked in on the other side of London. Think about what I've said.'

'I will,' Lily promised, rose and pulled her mum into a hug. 'Thank you for coming here.'

Her mind whirled as her mother clicked the door shut behind her. Emotions cascaded inside her. If she told Darius she loved him, she would have to trust him. As, perhaps, her mother should have trusted her father—trusted their love, trusted that love would trump everything else.

Darius watched the last board member leave the room and hoped he'd done enough to hold their confidence. He knew he'd fought his corner. Now, as and when Enzo's will went public and the story broke, he'd at least know he'd done all he could.

And that mattered. But just weeks ago it would have been *all* that mattered. Now, he missed Lily with a depth he wouldn't have believed possible. All he wanted to do was call her, see her, share the day's news with her, and the knowledge he couldn't was bleak. But it would fade. He'd throw himself into work, and surely he would stop thinking about her? There were reminders everywhere, despite the fact Lily had never even been here with him. All it took was a song, a scent of vanilla, the bar of black soap that he couldn't bring himself to throw away, the stars at night…

He looked up as the door opened, assumed it was someone who had thought of a final question.

But instead it was Gemma, and he rose to his feet.

'Gemma.'

'Darius.' His godmother came forward, approached him hands outstretched and enveloped him in a hug—the one person who had done that consistently in his life. 'How are you?' she asked.

'Good. The meeting went well and—'

His godmother cut across his speech without compunction. 'That's not what I meant. I have full confidence that you have everything covered on the work front. I meant how are you and Lily?'

He forced himself to meet her eye. 'We are trying to keep things going long-distance, but to be honest I think its fizzling out.' He tried a laugh. 'Probably all for the best. I'm not cut out for "long term".'

There was a pause and Gemma leant forward. 'That's not true,' she said. 'You're a good man and you are cut out for the long term. I've always known that and I've been waiting for the right person to come along. I thought Lily was that person.'

'She isn't.' He tried again. 'It was good while it lasted, but both of us are committed to our work, our businesses, and neither of us wants long-term commitment.'

Gemma eyed him narrowly. 'Then why do you look so miserable?' she asked gently. 'I can see it in your eyes, Darius, the same look you had as a little boy. Perhaps you do want more with Lily.'

'It wouldn't matter if I did.' He kept his voice steady, realising he might as well tell Gemma the truth. 'She doesn't want more with me. And that is fair enough.'

'And you're happy to let it go?' Gemma asked.

Darius looked at her in surprise. 'She made it clear it was over. She said it was better that way, that it was time to move on—that it was nothing personal but it was too risky to take things further.' His voice slowed down as he considered the words.

'Did you tell her how you feel?'

'I...' How did he feel about Lily? He pictured her—pictured holding her, kissing her, walking hand in hand with her; he felt the sense of connection, the sheer happiness of being with her and the ache of missing her.

He was a fool not to have seen it—he loved Lily. The idea was both glorious and terrifying, filling him with a sense of exhilaration. 'No, I didn't.' Euphoria faded as reality sank in. 'And I won't. How would that be fair to her, to tell her I love her? She wants to move on, I need to let her do that.'

'Or you could fight for her, try to win her love, make her see that you are worth the risk of hurt. But to do that you need to believe it yourself, Darius. I believe in you. I believe you are capable of commitment and love.'

Was he? He thought of Lily. He thought again

of her beautiful face, her smile, her warmth and compassion; thought about the sound of her laughter, the feel of her body against his, her hair against his chest. The way she'd listened to him, the way she'd held him. He would never hurt her; the knowledge was absolute and real. He would never abandon her.

And, damn it, she was worth fighting for. He'd given her a mealy mouthed offer of an extension of their fling, and shame ran through him at the memory. Lily was worth more than that, so much more, and he'd bottled it. He hadn't offered her his heart.

He rose to his feet, moved over to his godmother and hugged her. 'Thank you, Gemma. For being the best godmother a man could wish for.'

'You're welcome.'

Lily pulled the office door shut and set off towards the tube station. As she walked, she wondered if she'd made the right decision. Nerves skittered inside her even as she told herself she still didn't have to go through with it. She didn't have to catch the plane to LA the next day and, even if she did, she didn't have to go and see Darius. She hadn't told him she was coming. She could simply visit as a tourist and then return home. Or she could take her mother's advice, follow her heart and find the courage to tell Darius the truth. The idea, the sheer possibility, that she would see Darius filled her with a sense of anticipation and yearning...

Her thoughts broke off as she saw a man heading towards her, a tall, dark-haired man with an assured stride. Lily blinked, sure that it was another figment of her imagination. In the past days, she had 'seen' Darius so many times, only to get closer and realise it was nothing but a mirage.

Then... 'Lily.'

Her heart somersaulted, cartwheeled, and every muscle told her to run into his arms. But she forced herself to stay still and keep her face neutral, hoping he hadn't read her initial joy at seeing him.

'Darius. Is everything OK?'

He smiled at her, the smile tentative but warm, lighting his grey eyes. 'It is now,' he said. 'I was wondering, can we talk?'

Again her treacherous heart leapt and again she forced herself to stillness. This wasn't the scenario she'd planned. Perhaps he was here to discuss how to end their fake relationship.

'Of course,' she said, coolly. 'We can go back to my office or...'

'I've booked a table for dinner, if that's OK?'

'Dinner is fine.'

'Great.' Now his smile widened and she couldn't help it—she smiled back, even as she warned herself to take care.

They headed towards the road, both content with silence, a silence that strangely enough didn't feel awkward as he hailed a taxi and gave the address of a restaurant in Mayfair. Once they alighted, he gestured to a glass-fronted building. 'It's a Moroccan restaurant,' he explained. 'I've been missing Marrakesh.'

His words unfurled a small tendril of hope inside her and she allowed herself a small smile. 'So have I,' she said softly.

They entered and Lily blinked, trying to work out what was going on. There were no other diners, and the only illuminated part of the room was a table in the centre, with a chandelier overhead sending down a dim glow that showed a beautifully set table. It was strewn with rose petals and above the table was a massive helium heart-shaped balloon.

Lily gasped, trying to keep her voice level, trying to tell herself that this must be a set-up. Maybe in all the mixed emotions of the past days she'd quite simply forgotten that they'd arranged this. But then why had he asked if they could talk? 'I...don't understand,' she settled for. 'Is this...?'

'This is real,' he said. He stood and faced her and she could see the tension in his body, the set of his jaw, the deep intent focus in his eyes. 'One hundred percent real. I know it's a little late, but I am asking you if you will be my valentine—for as long as you want to be. I asked you here to talk but I want you to know from the get-go that I love you. I know you said that you want to move on, that you think this is too risky. I understand that. But you also said that it's not personal.'

He inhaled deeply. 'But it is personal and that's why I want to speak from my heart.' Just as she'd advised him to for his speech. 'I promise you that I will never intentionally hurt you, I will never leave you, I will never be unfaithful to you. I also know that those are words, words that anyone could say, but I mean every single one, and all I am asking is a chance to prove myself. We can take it as slowly as you like. I know trust had to earned, built up, but if you think there is any chance for us, any chance at all, then please say yes.'

Lily knew she should have broken in, should

have stopped him before now, reassured him, told him how she felt. But she hadn't been able to. She had been listening to the words with an ever-growing sense of elation, joy and happiness. Because she knew that, as he spoke, Darius would never make promises that he couldn't keep, or make a deal he couldn't honour.

'Yes,' she said. 'Yes, I will be your valentine. Your forever valentine. Because I love you too. With all my heart.'

'You do?' Happiness suffused his face, his smile the widest she'd ever seen. 'You're sure? You're not just saying that?'

'I'm not just saying that. Look…' She pulled out her phone. 'I booked a ticket to LA. I was coming to see you to tell you I love you.' The words tumbled out of her mouth as he led her over to a velvet two-person sofa pushed against one of the restaurant walls.

They sat and she took his hand in hers, never wanting to let go. 'I knew I loved you at the wedding but I never thought that you could possibly love me. That, even if you did how, could I trust it would last for ever? But you're right—it is personal. It's not about trusting love, it's about trusting you. And I do trust you.' With all her heart.

'And…' She took a deep breath. 'It was also about trusting myself. Believing in myself.'

He nodded, his grey eyes focused on her face, and she knew that he was listening, truly listening. 'And I found that concept hard—believing you could love me for ever.

'You see, when I was younger, Cynthia and Gina resented me because of what my mum had done to their lives. They decided to take it out on me. We were all sent away to boarding school and they…made my life miserable, bullied me.' Even now she could hear the near embarrassment in her voice, as if she had done something wrong.

'It wasn't your fault.' His voice was deep and reassuring, knowing unerringly the right thing to say.

'I know, and I thought I'd worked my way through it, and achieved success through work. But I think deep down all the insecurity was still there. Because the worst thing they did wasn't the physical actions, the chillies in my food or the slugs in my bed. It was how they made me feel—ugly and stupid and small. That's why I didn't tell anyone what was happening, or why I didn't tell you. I didn't want you to think of me as a small, pathetic victim.'

Darius pulled her close. 'I could never think

that of you. I have seen first hand how brave you are, how you stand up for others. I would never pity you, Lily; you are too courageous, too strong for that. But when I think of the young girl you were, and how you suffered, I am truly sorry—but it also makes my admiration for you all the greater for what you have achieved, the woman you are and the way you handled the wedding. Thank you for telling me now.'

'I'm telling you because I want you to know how much you have helped me overcome those insecurities. You make me feel beautiful and have allowed me to believe I am worthy of love. You've shown me that I can trust—trust you and trust our love.'

'And you have done the same for me. I refused to think a "for ever" love was possible for me because I was so so sure that my relationships with my parents, my upbringing, meant I would mess it up. You changed that, made me believe that I could, because I know with all my heart that my love for you is for ever and real. I know that for you I can be anyone. You listened to me, put things into perspective for me, made me see that maybe all the fault wasn't mine. That I am capable of love and being loved. Capable of being a good husband or father.'

'I know that you are. With all my heart.'

Now he dropped to one knee. 'Then please, Lily, give me the chance to be a good husband and father. Will you marry me?'

And out of his pocket came a jewellery box.

'Yes. Of course I will marry you...' Joy filled her—joy and happiness that soared through her veins along with a deep, enduring love for this man, a man whom she loved with all her heart.

She opened the box and gave a small gasp of delight. There winked up a diamond ring set with dark-blue gems in a star shape. 'To match your eyes,' he said as he slipped it onto her finger, then pulled her into his arms. And, as he kissed her in a glorious, head-spinning kiss, Lily thought she would burst with happiness.

When they finally stepped apart, he gestured to the table. 'And now I think it's time for champagne and food.'

She looked round the restaurant. 'How on earth did you manage this?'

Darius grinned. 'Once I realised I loved you, I knew I had to tell you. But I wanted to make it special. I found this restaurant, which is actually in the midst of renovations. I hired it for the week. Then I flew Jamal and his team across to make a celebratory dinner, if that was called for. They are in the kitchen waiting to be told what to do.'

Happiness bubbled inside her for this incredible, thoughtful man as they sat down at the table and raised their glasses to each other.

'And,' he said, 'I got you one more thing. Hold out your hand.'

She did and he placed something on her palm, something that made her heart overflow with love and laughter. There nestled in her hand was another charm for her bracelet—a Moroccan slipper.

'To symbolise our very own fairy-tale happy ending.'

And in that magical moment Lily knew this truly was happy ever after.

* * * * *

If you enjoyed this story, check out these other great reads from Nina Milne

Bound by Their Royal Baby
His Princess on Paper
Snowbound Reunion in Japan
Wedding Planner's Deal with the CEO

All available now!